In Sector 29, at "the Progress," the Princess mingled with the Galaxy's most eligible commoners to choose a Consort to rule with her. But one is a traitor, the instrument of a terrifying galactic conspiracy! Joined by the Roumeniers, their lifetime friends, Yvette and Jules D'Alembert secretly search the candidates, rushing against time to protect the life of their Princess.

Disguised as a country rube from a colony planet, Jules infiltrates the group and narrows his suspects to three—the arrogant Anton Borov from Kolokov; the enigmatic Aranian, Choyen Liu; and Paul Symond, the Princess's favorite! One is carrying a "time bomb," determined to destroy the succession. An unearthly murder betrays the killer and Jules confronts an uncontrollable and deadly fanatic!

AS AN UNKNOWN FORCE THREATENS THE SAFETY OF THE SUCCESSION OF EARTH'S EMPIRE, THE D'ALEMBERTS FACE THEIR MOST CHALLENGING SPACE ADVENTURE!

THE
CLOCKWORK
TRAITOR

E. E. "DOC" SMITH
with
Stephen Goldin

PYRAMID BOOKS NEW YORK

THE CLOCKWORK TRAITOR

A PYRAMID BOOK

Copyright © 1977 by Verna Smith Trestrail

Pyramid edition published January 1977
Second printing, April 1977

Library of Congress Catalog Card Number: 76-55127

Printed in the United States of America

Pyramid Books are published by Pyramid Publications (Harcourt Brace Jovanovich, Inc.). Its trademarks, consisting of the
word "Pyramid" and the portrayal of a pyramid, are registered
in the United States Patent Office.

PYRAMID PUBLICATIONS
(Harcourt Brace Jovanovich, Inc.)
757 Third Avenue, New York, N.Y. 10017

dedicated to my mother, Frances Goldin—
for the one that got away
S. G.

Prologue

Rawl Winsted's head felt bruised. It was not a physical feeling but a mental one, a fuzziness in his mind as though his entire brain were wrapped in cotton wool. And there was one particular portion of his memory that he simply could not touch. Every time he would send an exploratory thought in that direction it would dissipate into nothingness, leaving him with a feeling of mild confusion.

He knew precisely what was causing that sensation: a hypnotic block. It had been placed there to prevent him from knowing exactly why he had come to the planet Kolokov, whom he had worked for, and what he had done. He resented it a little—after all, what man liked having a portion of his life permanently taken away from him? To never know what he had done or said for a period of about a week was a slightly chilling concept.

But his resentment was slight. He had accepted the necessity for the hypnotic block as one of the conditions of his employment on the just-completed job. And besides, his employer—whoever it had been—had given him a substantial bonus for agreeing to the treatment. The thought of the extra ten thousand rubles tucked neatly away in his bank account was a very consoling one.

Even so, his thoughts could not help but be attracted to that blank spot in his mind, just like a tongue playing over the vacancy left by a recently extracted tooth.

He brought his mind back to the business at hand. Since

he was here on Kolokov anyway, he could not resist the temptation to make a little extra money, and the piece of jewelry on the worktable before him represented a sizeable investment that could pay off handsomely. It was a brooch that had been stolen two nights ago—gold set with several small diamonds in the center of a triangle of enormous emeralds. It was an expensive piece, but totally useless in its present form because it was an original and easily identifiable. He had paid the thief only two thousand rubles for it, which was less than half the value of the stones and the gold by themselves.

But when he was finished practicing his art, the piece could easily be worth five times what he had paid for it. Using ultraminiature equipment, he could alter some of the crystal striations in the stones so that even under radiometric tests they would not appear to be the stolen ones. The gold he would melt down and re-form into an entirely new structure, so beautiful it would command a fine price and so different that he could even sell it to its original owner without fear that it would be recognized.

This was Winsted's trade, and he was a master at it.

So intense was his concentration upon the brooch that it took him several seconds to realize that someone was knocking on the door of his rented studio. Concealment was second nature to him; he slipped the brooch into a secret pocket of his vest and walked cautiously to the door.

"Who's there?"

"Police, Gospodin Winsted. Open up at once."

Rawl Winsted knew a moment of blind panic. There was enough evidence in this room alone to send him to prison for twenty years. He fought at the mist that beclouded his mind, and then remembered that he had arranged a back exit to this room specifically against the possibility of being discovered. Without saying another word, he moved toward the concealing door that led to the crawlspace that in turn led to the roof, where his personal copter was waiting.

My mind is working slowly today, he thought as he crawled through the hatchway and pulled the door shut behind him. *Must be the aftereffects of the hypnotic block. But I'd better shake it off soon, or I'll be in real trouble.*

The police, he knew, would wait no more than thirty seconds outside the door before smashing it in and dis-

8

covering him missing. He had heard only the voice of one man outside the door, but there might be a second. Winsted doubted there would be any more than that—he was realistic enough to know that his own place in the hierarchy of crime did not warrant sending more than two policemen out after him. There was a very good chance, therefore, that his copter would be unguarded and that he'd be able to make his escape before they could catch him. He'd have to move quickly, though.

The rooftop seemed clear as he emerged from the crawl-way and began running across the open surface to his vehicle. He made it and slid into the pilot's seat just as two men came out of the elevator tube. Both had their stunners drawn and, as they caught sight of him, one dropped to his knees to fire while the other ran toward the copter. The first officer's stun-gun beam bounced harmlessly off the windshield of Winsted's vehicle as it began lifting rapidly into the air. The second man had dropped his stunner and had reached, instead, for his blaster. It was probably a low-powered field weapon, but even so it was something to respect.

Winsted changed all of his copter's acceleration from vertical to horizontal and skimmed sideways off the rooftop, avoiding the fire of the policeman who expected him to go upward. In doing so, Winsted narrowly avoided a collision with another copter coming in for a landing on the building next door. Swerving his vehicle around, the fugitive took off into the metropolitan sky, hoping to lose himself in the dense downtown air traffic.

As he flew, he kept a careful watch all about him. At first it seemed as though he had made a successful get-away; the radar screen showed no other vehicles at this altitude following him in the traffic pattern. But the policemen at the building must have recorded and broadcast his serial number, because from out of nowhere five copters surrounded him, paralleling his course—one below, one above, and three in a triangle around him at the same altitude.

The radio on his control panel came to life. "Land your craft at once, Winsted, or face the consequences. We have authorization to fire on your copter if necessary."

Think, man, Winsted told himself. But his mind still felt slightly muzzy from the hypnotic block and his thoughts jammed up against one another in a hopeless tangle. He knew there would be no way he could break out of this formation if the law officers were authorized to shoot—and he would not be likely to survive the crash that would follow their blasting his vehicle. He had no choice but to give in and hope to win his case in court.

"Acknowledged," he said in a weary tone as he began piloting his craft slowly down to a nearby rooftop. The copter under him got respectfully out of his way and the rest of the police followed him, maintaining a cautious distance.

Oh well, it could be worse, Winsted thought. *I've got a lot of money in the bank, I can afford a sharp lawyer. I may worm my way out of this yet.*

But Winsted's case was never to come to trial . . . and what began as a routine police arrest would shortly come to the notice of the Service of the Empire. The repercussions would be felt from the planet Kolokov all the way to Earth, and would threaten the stability of the succession to the very Throne of the Empire itself.

Chapter 1

The Princess's Progress

For Crown Princess Edna Stanley, heiress to the Throne of the Empire of Earth, there was little time for unhappiness. Her schedule was so filled with official duties that her own personal emotions had to wait. There was always some bridge to dedicate or a new starship to christen; there were endless testimonial banquets given in honor of this or that outstanding personage; there were school graduations at which she was requested to speak, charity benefits where the presence of a member of the Imperial Family would bring in more money for some worthy cause; there were art exhibitions and theater performances and sporting events that she, as a patroness of such activities, could not avoid. Also, her father insisted that she sit in and give advice at more and more meetings of the Imperial Council; in two more years she would be inheriting the Throne following his abdication, and he wanted to make certain that she was fit to govern the affairs of the Empire wisely. More and more often, he asked her to make the decisions in his place, to accustom her to the responsibility of power.

All of these things, and a myriad more besides, stole time away from the young woman's private life. If she had had any brothers or sisters it would have lightened the load, for they could have shared the duties. But there were no siblings. Her parents had thought it best to have only one child, and that fairly late in life; the history of the Stanley dynasty was replete with insurrections and conspiracies brought about by dissident family members.

11

Six previous Stanley rulers had been assassinated by their own relatives; the current Emperor and his wife wanted to spare their child the trauma of dealing with scheming siblings.

Edna Stanley sighed. Perhaps it was a blessing that she had been raised as an only child, without having to compete for so high a prize as the Crown. But it certainly was a mixed blessing, and one that left her no time for herself.

She had been moping around listlessly for a week before her mother spotted the change in her behavior and took her aside to talk to her.

"What's the matter, dear?" asked the Empress Irene.

"Nothing, really."

"Don't try to tell me that, I know you a little too well. Something is depressing you, and I'd like to know what it is."

Edna looked down at her feet, avoiding her mother's eyes. "It just all seems so pointless, somehow."

"What does?"

"All of it. The speeches, the handshakes, the aching feet, the boring dinners, the . . ." She stopped suddenly.

"Go on. I think you were getting to the important one."

"The Progresses." Edna's voice was tinged with sarcasm.

Light began to dawn inside the Empress's mind. "I see. And the fact that you're due to go on another Progress at the end of next week is making you feel depressed, is that it?"

"It wouldn't be so bad if anyone interesting went along. But they always choose such dull people. The men are always of two types—either the athlete with the flashy smile or the bookworm with the squinty eyes. I'm twenty-four years old; why can't they realize I'm looking for someone a little more balanced?"

Irene took her daughter's arm gently and led her over into one of the numerous alcoves in the Imperial Palace. The two women sat down on a bench and faced each other for a serious mother-daughter talk. "Each grand duke is responsible for the men you meet while on Progress through his Sector. They know how important it is that you find the right man, and perhaps they're being a little conservative. After all, they don't want to present anyone who'd be wildly *unsuitable*."

"It'd be a welcome change," Edna grumbled. "I just wish they'd give me more of a choice. I am old enough to make up my own mind."

"The Progresses can't be all that bad," the older woman said. "I seem to recall meeting your father on one, and it was a distinctly pleasant experience." She smiled warmly, recalling that happy time. It was obviously a cherished memory.

"I'm sure it was for you," her daughter answered. "You were a commoner then, selected to meet the Crown Prince, chosen out of I don't know how many thousands. It was a great honor for you, I'm sure, and I'm glad you went." She smiled at her mother. "I really do mean that. I couldn't have a better set of parents. But you really had to be something special for Father to pick you out of that crowd, because I'm sure it was no enormous honor for him to meet a group of commoners."

"You have to meet them sometime. Your father would like to see you marry before you ascend the Throne."

Edna nodded. The Stanley Doctrine, laid down by Empress Stanley Three, declared that members of the Imperial Family *must* marry commoners; that was done to insure a continuation of strong bloodlines and to avoid intermarriage solely within the nobility. And the only real chance she had to meet commoners at other than formal occasions was at these Progresses.

"I know, another of my royal duties. Don't worry, I won't shirk it. I only wish there were some way to keep them from being so dull."

"Oh, it won't be all that bad. You'll be spending the time at Cambria, won't you? You've always liked that place, ever since you first vacationed there as a small girl. And Sector Twenty-Nine has some interesting planets and people in it. I'm sure it won't be nearly as dull as you think it's going to be."

"You're probably right," Edna said, trying valiantly to give her mother a convincing smile. "I'm so used to going to dull ceremonies and dull banquets that I begin to think everything is going to be dull. At least it'll give me a chance to drop a lot of the formality. I need to relax and be myself."

But though her words were optimistic, inside she was still wondering how to avoid being bored to death.

Nearly fifty parsecs away, the subject of the Crown Princess's Progress was also on the mind of a young man waiting with more than a dozen others inside a plush office in the administration building of the duke of his planet. Magazines were scattered about the waiting room, but most of the young men were too nervous to read. This was the day of decision, and only one of them would be chosen to represent their planet in the Progress.

The door to the inner office opened and Gospodin Rhee's bald head poked out. He called out a name, and the young man in the corner looked up. It was *his* name; he was the chosen one. Struggling to maintain his appearance of outward calm, he rose to his feet and walked to the door of the inner office. He could feel the stares of the other applicants upon him, cold as winter clouds. All of them were thinking the same thought: The one who was picked was certainly no better than they were. Why was it him instead of them?

He went into the office with the bald man, shook hands, then sat down in the proffered chair. "Congratulations," Rhee said. "Out of better than fifteen hundred applicants, you have been selected to represent our world in the upcoming Progress."

"I'm honored, sir," said the young man. "I don't know what to say. I hardly think I'm worthy."

"Our computers say otherwise. They've decided you're the best eligible bachelor our planet can offer the Princess. In personality, intellect, and fitness you came out far superior to all the others. It's we who should thank you for representing us.

"*Khorosho*. Be that as it may, there are millions of tiny details to be taken care of, and only a short while to do them in. There are reams of papers for you to sign —purely formalities, of course. Part of your prize is that we will provide you with a whole new wardrobe, luggage, and travel accessories. We'll have to arrange for your passage to Ansegria, too. You're lucky, you know. All you had to do was compete with a lot of other men. You didn't have to fill out all the forms that went with it, like I did."

He sighed. "Well, we might as well get to it. Start

by signing these," and he handed the young man a thick sheaf of papers.

Half an hour later, the young man emerged from the building with his right hand sore from all the signatures he'd had to write. He flexed the muscles slowly as he walked out the door into the late afternoon sunlight.

He sensed, more than saw, the man coming up from behind him. A brown-cloaked figure slithered up out of the shadows and poked an object into his ribs. It felt suspiciously like the barrel of a gun. "Do just as I say," came a gravelly voice, "and you won't get hurt."

The young man was far from a coward, but he was not about to risk certain death by disobeying. "Whatever you say." He put his hands out slightly at his sides in a gesture of submission.

"Move toward that alley." The man with the gun gestured over to the right where a narrow corridor ran between two buildings. The young man walked in the indicated direction, with his kidnapper directly behind him. The gun never left the young man's ribs the entire time.

They walked some little distance into the alley until the dark shadows from the buildings completely hid them and they were out of sight of the street. "What do you want with me?" the young man finally dared to ask. His captor didn't answer, so he asked again, more loudly this time.

"Quiet!" came the muffled voice. Then, after a pause, it added, "You wouldn't understand."

The kidnaper, at this point, moved over beside him, and the gun barrel left his ribs for a moment. Deciding that this might be his only opportunity to put up a fight, the young captive swung into action. One of the reasons he had been picked for the Progress was that he was in top-notch physical condition and possessed lightning reflexes. With his left hand, he reached out to grab the gun from his captor while with his right he pulled off the cowl that had hidden the abductor's face.

From that point on, nothing went as he intended.

He had hit the other's gun hand fairly hard, he thought. The strength he'd put into the blow should at least have deflected his adversary's aim, if not knocked the blaster totally out of his grasp. Instead, his hand hit the other's and stopped there. The kidnaper's arm did not move in the slightest from its position, as though sheer physical strength kept it pointed straight at its intended victim. But the failure of that attack was only a minor surprise compared to what the young man saw as he ripped off the other's facial covering.

He found himself looking directly into his own face. His own eyes stared calmly back at him, his lips curled in a casual smile. There was now no attempt to disguise the timbre as the other said, in his own voice, "Yes, aren't the wonders of science marvelous?"

Then, before the young man could even cry out in his astonishment, his exact duplicate squeezed the trigger and a bolt of searing heat lashed out, burning a hole completely through the hapless young man's abdomen. He crumpled to the ground without ever having an answer to his unspoken question: Why?

The duplicate bent over him, clucking slightly and shaking his head. Then, with one casual gesture, he lifted the body over his shoulder as though it were a sack of feathers and continued walking down the alley to the spot where he'd parked his car. His business in this place was done.

And in the immense metal monolith that was known as Rimskor Castle, two other men were also engrossed in the subject of the Princess's upcoming Progress.

Duke Fyodor Paskoi of Kolokov was a skeleton of a man who looked as though he had no right to still be alive. He massed barely thirty-five kilograms, yet stood close to two meters tall. The skin was stretched taut over his bony frame, his tendons and ligaments were like tough cords, and he had no muscles to speak of. Veins stood out like enormous blue highways just under his skin. He resembled nothing so much as a stick figure a child might draw. What little hair he had on his head was confined to a few white wisps that straggled out from either side of his skull. His eyes were enormous orbs of white with small green irises and black pinpoints of pupils. They gleamed with the eerie glow of fanaticism.

But for all the horror of his appearance, Duke Fyodor was most definitely alive. Though he had contracted his rare and usually fatal illness as a child nearly thirty years

16

ago, he did not die of it. His father, the then duke, had spared no expense to ensure his survival and the survival of the family name. Prosthetic devices of every kind known to medical science of the twenty-fifth century kept him functioning.

Because his body was too weak to stand against the normal gravity of his planet, a mechanical exoskeleton supported him. Miniscule motors powered every movement of his limbs. A pacemaker regulated the beating of his weakened heart; in fact, machines controlled the activities of virtually all his internal organs. Even his teeth were artificial, as the real ones had fallen out long ago.

As life, it was pitiful; but as survival, it was a triumph.

His weak white eyes—aided by tiny, almost invisible lenses—scanned the note he had been handed and the news caused him to chuckle. It was an eerie sound, very much akin to a death rattle. "It's done," he said. "The substitution is complete." His voice was flat and buzzy, being electronically modulated; it emanated from twin speakers on either side of his head, giving authority to even his most trivial pronouncements.

The man with him, Dr. Immanuel Rustin, smiled. "Did Your Grace have any doubts about my abilities?"

"None whatsoever. I knew the man who designed this hell cage that keeps me alive could devise anything. But other factors than your abilities entered into this endeavor. We're playing the game for large stakes, my friend, and every moment must be considered critical. Detection at this stage would prove fatal."

"He will not be detected." Dr. Rustin, a small man with deep set, intense eyes and a beak of a nose, made one of his emphatic gestures with his arms. "Our little creation was built to perfection, even down to fingerprints, voice-print, and retinal patterns. Only an X ray would reveal his true nature, so stop worrying. They're not about to give him another medical exam—at least not for a while yet—and by that time we'll be in a position to fake the results."

"I know, I know, we've been all over this a thousand times before. It's just that all my life has been an uphill struggle; I could never afford to take anything for granted, and I don't intend to start now."

17

He stopped for a minute and gazed down at his companion, his eyes seeming to burn twin holes through the doctor's soul. "There's one thought I've been afraid to voice all this time, yet has me more worried than anything. What if *he's* wrong about the programming?"

There was no question in Rustin's mind about the antecedent of that pronoun. Only one person was spoken about in those reverent tones—their mysterious superior, known to them only as "C." "Has *he* ever been wrong before?"

The Duke raised a hand to finger the little integrated circuit chip he wore on a golden chain around his neck.

"No," he admitted, "it's uncanny, but *he's* never been wrong . . . yet. I don't know what *his* source of information is, but there are times *he* seems to know everything in the entire empire."

"So trust in *him*," Rustin soothed. "*He* says that the physical body plus the personality we programmed into our robot will be precisely what Princess Edna will fall in love with and want to marry. In two years she will rule the Empire—and our robot will be her consort." He smiled. "It's as I've told you on so many occasions: we're planting a time bomb against the Princess—and against the Imperial Family itself."

"But to what purpose? That's what disturbs me sometimes at night, before the sedatives put me out completely. We've worked for years getting this just right, always on *his* orders, and yet we have no more idea of the ultimate goal than we did when we started. For what purpose does *he* want to rule the Empire?"

"Why does *anyone* want to?" Rustin shrugged. "I know I wouldn't want that responsibility. Frankly, I don't care. We've been rewarded well so far, and we've been promised even greater rewards in the future. I shan't question it. If you're so curious, you ask *him;* it's almost time, you know."

"Yes, that's why I'm so nervous. Our job is technically done, now; I'm wondering what comes next."

Over against a wall, a readout screen flashed into life. The telecom unit was hooked into a computer terminal, and it was through this linkage that they received their orders. They had never seen or spoken to their enigmatic boss, and had no idea who he (or she) might be. The mechanical exoskelton that supported Duke Fyodor's fragile body moved quickly over to view the one word that the screen had printed on it:

REPORT.

Duke Fyodor did so, as concisely and accurately as possible. His mechanically aided fingers moved slowly and uncertainly over the keyboard as he typed; his exoskeleton, while perfectly mobile, was not as dextrous as he would have liked it to be. When he finished his report, he typed in the end code and waited for "C's" response.

The answer came back within a minute. Fyodor stood over the teletype, reading each word as it printed out on the screen. Even after the message had stopped, he stood silently for a long moment, staring at the machine.

"Well," Rustin said, "don't keep me in suspense. What does it say?"

Duke Fyodor laughed. It was not a pleasant sound. "All that worry for nothing," he said, punching for a printout of the message and handing the paper to his companion. Then he walked out of the room.

Dr. Rustin took the sheet of paper and studied it, perplexed. The message written on it was simple and direct:

CONGRATULATIONS, JOB WELL DONE. THERE WILL BE NO FURTHER COMMUNICATION UNTIL AFTER THE SUCCESS OF THE PLAN.

C.

As always, Rustin burned the message.

Chapter 2

"Time Bomb"

Each of the thirty-six Sectors into which all of human-occupied space was divided was administered from Earth, the seat of Imperial government. Since most Sectors contained several dozen inhabited planets apiece, the administrative problems were immense, requiring an elaborate bureaucratic structure to handle the myriad problems that could arise among so many peoples. Each Sector had a Hall of State on Earth staffed by thousands of civil servants.

The Hall of State for Sector Four was bigger than most. Ostensibly, the reason for this was that Sector Four had a much larger number of planets to govern—upwards of a hundred, in fact. Located in Miami, Florida, North America, the building towered ninety-three stories high, dwarfing all others around it. And while it was true that a goodly percentage of the people working there were ordinary bureaucrats, there was a much stronger reason why not only the Hall of State itself, but all the smaller buildings surrounding it for a two-block radius—buildings which supposedly housed innocuous businesses—were crammed with people and computer equipment. This building was, in fact, the top secret headquarters for the Service of the Empire, or SOTE.

Even at night, the building was well lighted, for the Service could never sleep. Being ultimately responsible for the internal security of the entire realm, it could not afford to. Lights could be seen on in offices at almost any hour —particularly in one well-appointed office on the thirty-first floor.

A small jet vehicle zoomed in toward the roof of that impressive building. The edifice's defenses were such that even so small an aircraft was constantly in gunsight, but no action was taken against it. This vehicle was cleared for landing, and its occupants were two people who, for security's sake, could never be allowed to be seen entering through the front door.

The small jet—actually a Mark Forty-One Service Special camouflaged to look like a sports model Frascati groundcar—landed expertly on the flat rooftop and two people, a man and a woman, got out. Without bothering to look around—they knew they were as safe here as anywhere in the Universe—they walked straight to the door of an elevator tube and stepped inside. The air solidified beneath their feet and dropped them gently down sixty-three levels, where a set of doors opened in front of them and they stepped out.

At first glance, neither Jules nor Yvette d'Alembert looked like what they actually were—the two top agents in the entire SOTE network. Neither fitted into the tall, sleek image that the words "secret agent" conveyed to the public mind. Brother and sister were short and chunky; draft horses rather than thoroughbreds. But that first glance would be deceiving.

True, both of them were shorter and more massive than normal Earthers, but that was because they came from very special stock. The d'Alembert family came from the planet DesPlaines, where the gravity was slightly more than three times as strong as Earth normal. To survive under such harsh conditions, a person had to be built close to the ground; even a slight stumble could have serious consequences in so powerful a field. Tall people just did not survive long on DesPlaines.

But even beyond the strength and quickness of reflexes they shared with other natives of their world, Jules and Yvette d'Alembert had more specialized qualities going for them—for up until a year ago, they had been the star aerialists of the Circus of the Galaxy, skilled athletes with physical agility honed to absolute perfection by a lifetime of rigorous training.

The Circus of the Galaxy was virtually synonymous with the Family d'Alembert. That clan had founded the show several centuries ago, and it had continued to be mainly a family enterprise, with nearly a thousand d'Alemberts making up the current troupe. The Circus was managed by Etienne d'Alembert, who also happened to be the duke of the entire planet of DesPlaines. Running the Circus was so much more in his blood, though, that he left the administration of his world in the more than capable hands of his eldest son, Robert.

Managing the Circus was a full-time job, for more than one reason—for in addition to being the most popular single attraction in the entire Empire, the Circus was also the most powerful and versatile weapon in SOTE's considerable arsenal. Consider: it could and did travel anywhere in the Galaxy without arousing suspicion. Most planets, in fact, were overjoyed when the Circus decided to visit them. The personnel were all extremely agile, extremely talented in any number of areas—and extremely loyal to the Empire. Almost since its inception, the Circus had been the unofficial right arm of SOTE's intelligence-gathering network.

And of all the hundreds of d'Alemberts currently serving with the Circus, none surpassed in ability the two who had just emerged from the elevator tube. Yvette and Jules d'Alembert, the second and third children respectively of Duke Etienne, were, as far as the Service of the Empire was concerned, the perfect secret agents.

"Hello," Jules said as he walked through the doors of the elevator into the plush office beyond. "It's good to see you again."

"And it's good to know you've got some more work for us," Yvette added with a smile. "I hate just sitting around."

The office they had entered was obviously one belonging to an important executive. The floor was carpeted with a thick brown rug, the walls were paneled with beautifully grained solentawood and the beamed ceiling was also of that same rich wood. The large solentawood desk that faced the elevator was, as usual, nearly buried in mountains of paperwork, while behind it, inlaid in the wall and dominating much of the room, was the gold-crowned Shield of Empire. The enormous double-headed eagle cast its all-seeing gaze over everything in the room. The large picture window that overlooked Miami and the Atlantic Ocean was covered—there was no point to risking having the d'Alemberts' identities learned through telephone pictures that could be taken up to a kilometer away.

The man behind the desk stood up to greet them. He was dressed conservatively in a gray overtunic and slacks. The tunic was of the slightly-out-of-date high-collar fashion, and was fastened at the neck with an ornate platinum pin. The man's head was almost completely bald and the face was creased with lines of worry and responsibility, making him look much older than his forty-seven years. His eyes, though, were bright with life, and behind them glowed a force of intellect so strong that anyone would know this was a very special man.

And indeed he was special. He was Grand Duke Zander von Wilmenhorst, the ruler of the vast Sector Four, one-half Stanley blood, fifth in line of succession, and considered one of the most important men in the Galaxy. But what added to that importance—more than most people knew—was that he was also the head of SOTE, the man responsible for the peace and internal security of the Empire. As such, he was an intimate counselor and most trusted adviser to His Imperial Majesty Stanley Ten.

There was no trace of pomp or formality in his manner, though, as he rose to greet his two top agents. "How are you both?" he asked warmly, his interest genuine. He spoke, as they had, in Empirese, the Russian-English mixture that was the Galaxy's official tongue.

"Keeping in shape," Yvette replied. "We've had a nice rest back on DesPlaines since our last assignment, but it's been too long—and unless you give us some work, we don't have anything to do."

"There's not really even any room for us in the Circus anymore," Jules said wistfully. When he and his sister had graduated up to their present roles, their star spots were filled by their younger cousins, also named Jules and Yvette, so the outside world did not even know they had left.

The Head smiled as he came around from behind his desk to kiss Yvette politely on the cheek and shake Jules's hand firmly. "It never fails to amaze me," he said, "how eager the two of you are to risk your lives. If I had fifty more agents like you, I could retire and know the Empire

23

was still safe. Come on in and be seated; I'll fix you something to drink."

Yvette looked around, startled. "Where's Helena? Doesn't she usually tend to details like that?"

The person referred to was the Head's daughter, Duchess Helena von Wilmenhorst, who acted as her father's girl Friday. It was Helena who normally handled the routine matters in the Head's office.

"She's been much too overworked lately, so I gave her a month's vacation," their boss told them. "It's a luxury I can never afford anymore, but she's young and there's no reason why she should stay cooped up with business matters. Let her live a little first." He moved over to the bar and filled two glasses with ice.

"What she'd really like," Yvette said, "is for you to give her a field assignment. She's dying to get out there and prove herself." She watched as the older man poured each d'Alembert a tall glass of orange juice. DesPlainian bodies did not tolerate alcohol very well and, as health-conscious as the two agents were, they were very careful what sorts of stimulants they put into their systems.

"Absolutely out of the question," the Head said, bringing the glasses over to them. "I've got plenty of field agents; what I need most is someone around the office I can depend on. You've no idea what hell it is trying to keep the Service running efficiently. Besides," he lowered his voice to conspiratorial tones, "I'm training her to take over as Head when I retire. Nothing immediate, of course—but then, she's got a lot to learn, too."

"We rather thought you had something like that in mind" Jules grinned. "I think she'll do a good job, if and when."

"Please don't tell her about it," their superior cautioned them. "If she knew what she was really being trained for, she'd become self-conscious and freeze up. I want her limber enough to still learn."

"We understand," Yvette winked. "And we wouldn't dream of telling her. What else are *secret* agents for?"

"Ah, yes." Having served them their drinks, the Head returned to the big chair behind his desk and sat down. "About that. You know I have another assignment for you; much as I like you both, I can't just go summoning you to my office anytime I like. It's another luxury I

24

can't afford. You know, I presume, that the Princess is going on a Progress next week."

"Yes, that's no secret," Yvette said. "The newsrolls have been full of almost nothing else for weeks. Sector Twenty-Nine is hosting it this time, I believe."

"Correct. I'm glad you keep up with things. I have what may be an extremely easy and pleasant assignment for you this time—you are both to go along with the Princess and keep her safe."

Jules's eyes narrowed. "By that, I presume you are expecting that this will not be just an innocent little social affair."

"Right again, unfortunately. We have only the faintest of clues to go on, and it may mean nothing at all, but with the heiress's life at stake, we can't afford to take chances."

"I'd heard," Yvette said slowly, "that she was going to the planet Ansegria and would be staying with Baron Piers and Baroness Ximena of Cambria. I've met both of them and they're delightful people. Surely you don't suspect them of plotting anything, do you?"

"Let me start at the beginning," the Head sighed. "About a week ago, on the planet Kolokov, the local police picked up a man named Rawl Winsted on suspicion of accepting stolen property. On checking their files, they learned that Winsted was an interstellar fugitive and so, as a matter of routine, they transferred him over to SOTE's custody.

"Winsted, it seems, had quite a record. He was a jeweler by training and a crook by instinct. His normal line of business was to disguise jewelry, watches, what have you, to look like other things. Thieves would bring him their loot which is too well known to sell as is, and he would rearrange it—for a fee. Supposedly, he was an expert at working with miniature components." The Head sighed again. "We live in an age of specialization, that's for certain. As our methods for tracking stolen property become more sophisticated, so do the crooks' methods for hiding it.

"At any rate, the local branch of the Service began questioning him. They were hoping to discover as many of his previous contacts and associates as possible so that they could begin tracking down the loot he'd rearranged. Winsted was very closed-mouthed, but eventually they pried him open a little and discovered a secret infinitely more valuable than what they were seeking. There had been a hypnotic block placed in his mind concerning the reason he'd come to Kolokov in the first place."

Both d'Alemberts looked interested. A hypnotic block was a form of mental conditioning that prevented a person from remembering—except under the most illegal of inducements—the information that was within the block. It was an expensive and cumbersome treatment, and was only worth doing to hide information of the most crucial sort.

The Head noted their expressions. "I see it's piqued your curiosity, too. Yes, the chief of the local branch was also wondering why someone would go to all the trouble and expense of blocking that information. Certainly it wouldn't be merely to cover up the details of a jewel robbery—and besides, there hadn't been any thefts that major in the area for quite some time.

"The chief started to intensify her questioning. She used everything at her disposal short of nitrobarb and got the block open just a crack—but it was a vital crack. A phrase Winsted had heard had stuck in his mind: 'a time bomb against the Princess.' "

Both Jules and Yvette tensed. Their loyalty to the Crown was so deeply instilled that the mere mention of treason chilled them to the bone. The fact that the Princess happened to be a friend of theirs added to the sensation of horror.

"Of course," their boss went on, "that added a whole new dimension to the picture. Treason is something that's anathema to all of us, or we wouldn't be in the Service. The chief on Kolokov overreacted, I'm sorry to say. She beamed a message directly back here to me, which was the exact proper thing to do, but then she got a little impatient. Before I could reply—with Helena gone, I was backlogged with work—she took it on her own authority to give Winsted a shot of nitrobarb."

Yvette nodded. She was trained in the use of that drug, the most powerful truth serum yet discovered. It was impossible for anyone to lie or cover up facts under its influence, even people under hypnotic blocks. Unfortunately, the drug had a very bad side effect—namely, a 50 percent mortality rate. It was this fact that had placed the drug on the proscribed list; mere possession of it was a capital offense, though that did not stop a lot of people on both sides of the law from using it.

"Unfortunately," the Head continued, "she was not an expert and could not even spot Winsted's allergy to it. He died writhing in agony thirty minutes later, and she learned nothing further from him."

Again Yvette nodded. She had administered nitrobarb herself on a couple of occasions and knew exactly how tricky a thing it could be. For someone not completely trained in its use it was almost the equivalent of putting a blaster to the suspect's head and pulling the trigger.

"I couldn't fault her motives," the Head said, his voice calm and level. "But I had to reprimand her, anyway. Her rash action has placed the Princess in jeopardy. If she had waited another day or two, we could have dispatched an expert to either dismantle the block or use the nitrobarb in a more judicious manner, and we would have learned more, if not all, of the story. As it is, we've blown our one lead and we're back in the dark once more. You now know as much as we do."

"A time bomb," Jules mused. "But that's so general a threat. How can you be so sure that it will happen during the Progress?"

"I can't," the Head admitted. "I can only go on hunches and guesswork. There may be nothing to the threat at all, just something Winsted heard mentioned as a possibility. But, of course, we have to act on the assumption that the threat is real. If so, where could such a bomb be? The Imperial Palace or any of the various courts are out; they're so well guarded it would be next to impossible for anyone to sneak a time bomb in there. And remember, it was specifically said to be 'against the Princess.' The only certain way of getting her and not someone else would be to place the bomb in her rooms; again, our security is too tight for that.

"But in just seven days she goes on her Progress, to a place where the security is less stringent. If anyone were going to use a time bomb, that would be the place to do it."

"I presume the Baron's castle at Cambria has been checked out?" Jules asked.

"Top to bottom. Most discreetly, of course—we didn't

want to alarm the Baron and Baroness. Nothing was found, which only means that the bomb hasn't been placed yet. We'll need continual surveillance to make sure it never is. That's why I want the two of you along—you've got sharper eyes and quicker reflexes than anyone else available."

"Why not just cancel the Progress?" Yvette asked.

"That would be the simplest way, yes. But not necessarily the smartest. Remember, it was only a fluke that brought about this discovery, so that we know a tiny smidgen of the enemy's plans. Hopefully, he doesn't know that we know yet; Winsted was probably just a small cog in the plot and won't be missed. If we cancel the Progress now, our opponent will know we suspect something, and he'll change his plans. We might not learn about the next one until it's too late. We have to go with what we've got."

"What about following up with an investigation on Kolokov?" Jules suggested. 'Maybe we should try to find out what Winsted was doing there."

"I've already thought of that," said the Empire's master strategist. "The Circus is already on its way there; I trust your father and the rest of your family to find out what we need to know. But I want the two of you with the Princess. You're the best I've got, and she'll need your brains and agility on her side."

"Time bombs come in all sizes, shapes and colors," Yvette said. "And we won't have the faintest idea of what we're looking for."

"Exactly," their boss said with a grimace. "Winsted, remember, was an expert at working with miniature components. It's quite possible that he was called in on this job because of his talents—in which case, the bomb could be quite small indeed. It might be a small article by itself, or it could be a small part of some larger thing. You'll have to suspect everything that comes in contact with the Princess. You'll be given some sensor equipment that may help, but it'll be impossible to use it on absolutely every object. You'll have to go largely on instinct."

"Edna knows we'll be along, doesn't she?" Yvette asked.

"Certainly. I couldn't hold anything like this back from her. She had to okay the plans, as did her father. In fact, Edna said she's looking forward to meeting the two of you again, though she wishes the circumstances were more pleasant."

"So do we," Yvette agreed.

"What are our cover identities to be?" Jules asked.

"You'll both be part of the Princess's official retinue of bodyguards; only you and she will know you're anything more."

Jules shook his head. "I'm not sure if that's the best way. Uh, not that I mean to question your plans or anything," he added hastily.

"Question away. You're the one who has to do the actual work. I trust your instincts. If you can think of a better way, I'll be happy to hear it."

"Well," Jules began hesitantly, "if the bomb isn't in the castle now, it'll have to be brought in."

"My brother has a way with these brilliant deductions," Yvette said, smiling.

Jules ignored her interruption. "Whoever brings the bomb in knows that the Princess has bodyguards as a matter of routine. He will already have taken them into account, and will have some plans for eluding them. We might have a chance to see more if we're in a less official capacity."

The Head thought on that for a second. "What do you suggest, then?"

"The whole purpose of the Progress, really, is for the Princess to meet some commoners so that she can select her future husband. There will be many men there about whom we know very little."

"Actually, we know more about them than we do about most people. They've each had to undergo a thorough computer screening before they were picked. Theoretically they're all beyond reproach."

"Again, can we take that chance? It seems to me that they might be the weak link. They would have the best opportunity to bring in a bomb and place it near the Princess."

"And since the candidates don't know one another yet," Yvette said, picking up on her brother's reasoning, "you could pretend to be one of them and keep an eye on them."

"Exactly," Jules agreed.

"And I could be a lady-in-waiting," Yvette went on. "It

sounds an awful lot more pleasant than 'bodyguard,' and I could be just as close to her, if not closer. No one would suspect a thing."

The Head smiled. "I knew I chose the right people. In less than half an hour you're already taking charge and making this case your own. Yes, your suggestions make excellent sense and we'll follow through on them immediately. Work up whatever cover identities you want and I'll see that they're substantiated." He peered at their faces and noticed that there was still the slightest hesitation in Jules's face. "Anything else?"

"Well, on something like this, I'm not sure the two of us could cover absolutely everything. Would you mind if we brought in more help?"

"Who do you have in mind?"

Jules looked to his sister. "Do you think Vonnie and Jacques would be interested?"

"Mais oui! They'd be delighted." Her eyes narrowed as she smiled at her brother. "And, of course, you would have no great objections to working with Vonnie."

"None at all," Jules grinned back, then turned to the Head. "Yvonne and Jacques Roumenier."

"A good choice," their superior nodded. "Both top-notch agents. Of course, with her being your fiancée I'd almost suspect a little nepotism . . ."

"Like with you and your daughter? Sorry, sir, but Vonnie is about the best for the job."

"You should let an older man finish a sentence. I was about to say, 'but knowing you that's impossible.' Besides, the Roumenier family has turned out agents almost consistently as good as the d'Alemberts. When the families are that good, who minds a little nepotism? Sure, have them come along. They can fill the bodyguard posts that you two were originally scheduled for, and both of you can handle your own disguises."

He reached into a drawer of his desk and pulled out a medium-sized box. "This contains sensor equipment that might help you spot the bomb, as well as bookreels of the dossiers on the candidates the Princess will be meeting. Maybe you can find some clue in there that our own people missed." He handed the box to Jules and went to the bar to pour himself a glass of water; it was too late

30

at night, and he had too much work still to do, to fog his mind with alcohol.

"I know you realize this already," the Head concluded, "but I can't stress it enough. The safety of Crown Princess Edna is of the utmost importance. In two years, when her father plans to abdicate, she will be crowned Empress Stanley Eleven. She is the only child of her parents. If anything should happen to her, it would throw the entire succession into doubt. Theoretically there are other people in a neat line—I'm one myself—but that procedure has fortunately never been tested. If a crisis should arise, the entire Galaxy could dissolve into civil war. Keep that in mind—and keep Edna safe."

He raised his glass in the traditional Service salute: "Here's to tomorrow, fellows and friends. May we all live to see it!"

Chapter 3

Arrival at Rockhold

"If any one of these guys is a traitor," Yvette said with disgust, "I'll eat this entire bookreel."

The two d'Alemberts had stayed up the entire night viewing the files on the commoners the Princess was scheduled to meet less than a week from now. With time so short, there was little of it they could waste.

"It would be hard to find a more loyal lot," Jules admitted, munching on an apple. Thirteen commoners, each the pride of his respective world. Screened by computer for only the best qualities—or whatever the computer programmer thought the best qualities were. But they're all honest, all loyal, all intelligent. . . ."

"All handsome," Yvette put in.

"Really? I didn't notice."

"Someone had to. You don't expect a princess to hobnob with a gaggle of wumpmugs, do you?"

"*Eh bien,* so what does that prove?"

"It proves that you may have a bit of a problem blending in with such a group."

"Vonnie hasn't complained about my looks."

"Vonnie's lapses in taste are her own affair. But seriously, you will have a bit of an identification problem. There are thirteen male candidates, one from each inhabited planet in Sector Twenty-Nine. While none of them knows any of the others, they do know that there should only be a baker's dozen of them. They can all count to fourteen; how will you explain the extra one?"

"Simple. I'm from Julea, an experimental colony that's just getting started. We're not much yet, just a few thousand people, mostly agricultural types. Nothing exciting, which is why they haven't read about us in the newsrolls. I'll play a real rube—not overly bright, a little slow on the uptake...."

"Typecasting."

Jules was used to his sister's friendly jibes, and paid it no notice. "If one of the candidates is our bomber, I may be able to lull him into a false sense of security."

Yvette nodded slowly. "It may work. But if our bomber isn't in your crew, I may have my work cut out for me. I'll have to stick with Edna every second—which won't be easy, considering these events are designed to let her be alone with as many of the men as she can. How else is the poor girl to find out anything about them?"

"She can read their dossiers, like we have. They're so complete I feel as though I've known each of these men all my life."

"And speaking of getting to know them, *mon frère,* hadn't you better light a fire under your tail? The candidates will be assembling on Ansegria by now, and you don't want to be too late or you'll arouse suspicion."

"*Au juste.* I'll take the *Comet* and flash on out there, while you can follow along with the Princess's party. I'll leave the minor details up to you. You can message Vonnie and Jacques and tell them to meet you on Ansegria—it's faster than having them come all the way to Earth and then leaving again immediately. Oh, and you'd better send word along to the Baron and Baroness that we'll be there under cover—part of a routine precaution, tell them. No point in alarming them unduly."

"Will do. Now—get moving, and good luck."

Cambria was a coastal city bordering on the planet Ansegria's largest ocean. It was known primarily as a resort town, and was noted throughout Sector Twenty-Nine for the beauty and grandeur of its setting. It was replete with rolling hills and lush vegetation, blue skies, and always moderate weather. It was a large, sprawling city of low buildings and one-story houses spaced comfortably apart from one another. Its beaches were clean and unpolluted, with high, white cliffs coming sometimes to with-

33

in fifty meters of the waterline. Sea birds flew constantly overhead, their raucous cries a part of Cambria's enchanted atmosphere.

Rockhold Castle, home of the Baron and Baroness of Cambria, was located slightly outside the city proper at the edge of a high cliff overlooking the shore. It was an imposing stone edifice with a three-story building in the center, surrounded on three sides by a wide courtyard and only the barest indications of a wall, for form's sake. At the back of the building was nearly a full hectare of beautifully landscaped and terraced gardens. As the Baron and Baroness were fond of entertaining, there were plenty of accommodations within the castle itself for the number of guests the Princess's Progress would bring. The cost of the Progress was being defrayed by Grand Duke Manuel of Sector Twenty-Nine.

Jules had left his private ship, *La Comète Cuivré*, at the nearest spaceport in Canyonville and had driven to the castle in the same Mark Forty-One Service Special he had used for calling on the Head. Not only was the vehicle designed as both a groundcar and personal jet, but it snugged neatly into place with the d'Alemberts' two-person starship —ensuring that they always had good transportation whenever they needed it.

Being on the guest list, Jules was instantly admitted inside the castle's walls after a quick fingerprint and voiceprint check confirmed his identity. There were already a large number of cars parked in the courtyard, indicating that the rest of the candidates had already arrived. Jules parked his own car in the nearest available space, picked up his suitcase, and stepped out into the bright Cambrian sunlight.

His clothing matched precisely the character he wanted to portray. It was not very expensive—his home planet was ostensibly poor and would not be able to outfit him as lavishly as the others—and was about two years out of style. The brown velvet slacks were baggy and came only down to just above his ankles, exposing a trifle more of the boots than was customary. The gold brocade shirt was a trifle too gaudy to completely match the pants, and the ruffles were slightly overornate down the front. The sleeves reached only to the wrists, and had a tendency to ride up when he moved his arms. The leather vest was too tight, and cut slightly askew so that its fit was noticeably off. Jules's short brown hair was combed straight down over his forehead in a rustic manner. All in all, he was the country bumpkin spruced up for a date with his lady love, not half ready to be introduced to the Crown Princess of the Empire.

Jules carried his bag up to the main door, which was opened by a gaunt bearded man with a dour expression. "Hi there, Your Honor," Jules grinned at him. "I'm John Dallum, the candidate from Julea. I think you're expecting me."

"I am not His Honor, merely the steward," the man replied with an inborn sense of dignity. "His Lordship regrets that he cannot greet you in person, but has instructed me to show you to your quarters and introduce you to your fellow candidates." He made no move to take Jules's one overstuffed suitcase from him as he continued, "Follow me."

Jules was led upstairs to the second floor and down a long corridor thickly carpeted and lined with paintings of various seascape scenes. The room he was shown to was small, perhaps, for a castle but large by his own personal standards. It had a full-sized bed with nightstands and lights on either side, a long dresser with a large mirror, a walk-in closet that took up one entire wall, three chairs, a sensable booth, and a door that led into a private bathroom.

Jules gawked admiringly. "This sure is some layout you've got here."

"Thank you, sir. You will find the other candidates gathered in the day room." And the steward told him how to find that place, then left—ignoring Jules's awkward attempt to tip him.

Confident, then, that his new persona would pass muster, Jules unpacked quickly and hurried down to the day room, eager to meet the other men—and, perhaps, the prospective bomber. He walked with quick, ground-devouring steps, the pace of a man made bold by his own ignorance. He walked brashly through the double doors into the day room, stopped and faced the thirteen other men with whom he was "competing."

All of them were taller and better dressed than he was. They sat or stood around in small clumps, obviously en-

35

gaged in routine conversations except for one young man seated by himself in the corner. All of them stopped what they were doing as Jules entered so that they could size up his potential threat to their own chances of winning the Princess's favors. After one glance, it was obvious that most of them considered him no threat at all.

"Hi there," Jules beamed his standard, overly friendly greeting at them. "I'm John Dallum from Julea."

A tall, pleasant-looking chap came over and shook his hand. "Pleased to meet you. I'm Paul Symond from Lateesta." His grip was firm and decisive, his smile friendly, his voice warm. Jules decided right away that he liked this man.

"Come along," Symond continued. "I'll introduce you to the others." Then, having made himself Jules's unofficial escort, he led the SOTE agent around the room, naming the names that Jules already knew but had to pretend he didn't.

As they approached one tall, dark-haired man, Symond said, "This is Anton Ilyich Borov from the planet Kolokov. Anton, this is. . . ."

"Yes, I know," said the Kolokovnik with a faint sneer. " 'John Dallum from Julea,' wherever the hell that is. Yes, he made himself abundantly conspicuous on his arrival."

Jules knit his brow in puzzlement. "Did I do something to offend you, Gospodin Borov?"

"It's not what you've done, really, it's what you are. Here we all are, contestants for the hand of the next Empress of the Galaxy. We're supposed to be suave, courtly, gallant . . . then you come in here and turn this whole thing into a joke."

"I'm sorry, Comrade, but we don't have much time to learn elegant manners on Julea—we're too busy trying to stay alive. A colony planet is a hard place for survival, and we've all got to work hard just to eat."

Borov looked as though he were struggling to hold down further nasty remarks and take a more diplomatic approach. After a moment he smiled and offered Jules his hand. "Please don't misunderstand me, Dallum; there's certainly nothing sinful about the way you earn your living. I'm sure you're a very nice fellow, and I didn't mean any of what I said as personal invective. If I've inadvertently insulted you, then please accept my deepest apologies. But you must realize that the Princess is used to certain standards at the Imperial Court—standards which you, simply *because* you come from a colony planet, could hardly be expected to match. You just seem out of place here, and I question the wisdom of the Progress Committee in placing you with our group."

Jules shook hands with him, meanwhile eyeing the bigger man critically. Being from Kolokov, the planet where the time bomb conspiracy was supposedly hatched, Borov was the most likely suspect as the potential assassin. The SOTE agent tried to recall what the files had said about him. Borov was a champion chess player, president of a debating society and an amateur boxer and weightlifter. He came from a wealthy family; his mother ran one of the most influential financial consultant firms on Kolokov. Borov had seldom lost out on anything he'd ever wanted, and the computer personality profile did admit that he had a tendency to be overbearing. That, and a short temper, were considered his main weak points, but he had still ranked above everyone else on his planet and so had been selected to join the Progress. Jules made up his mind that this was definitely a man to watch.

"Oh, don't mind him," Symond said, taking Jules's arm and leading him further around the room. Then, in a lower, more private, tone, he added, "I think Borov is a little too filled with his own self-importance for his own good. In fact, from what I hear, the Princess actually has a preference for the short, dark types. You may actually stand more of a chance than a tall, blond, blue-eyed lunk like me. Come on, the rest of the guys aren't half that bad."

One by one, Jules was introduced to the rest of the candidates, and he had to agree that they were all an affable group of men; any of them would make admirable companions on a sports team or good company for sitting around and conversing about life and love. The atmosphere was definitely like a country club, a sociable setting for sociable people to get together and enjoy themselves.

The last man Symond introduced him to was Choyen Liu from the planet Anares. Liu was only slightly taller than Jules himself, though much slimmer and more delicate. His Oriental features made a nice contrast to the deep blue brocade of the robes he wore, the native dress of his home world. Anares had been settled three centuries

37

before by a group of mystics and, with some modifications, the religious philosophies had remained to this very day. Anarians didn't travel much, and so remained largely a mystery to the outside Universe.

"Hi," Jules said upon being introduced to this strange man. He stuck out his hand to shake Liu's, and the Anarian took it with a grip so strong that Jules was genuinely surprised. It nearly crushed him to his superstrong bones, yet there was no sign of either animosity or strain on the man's face. Jules was tempted to squeeze back with his DesPlainian strength, which would be sure to shatter the other's hand, but then thought better of it; it would be out of character. So instead he pulled his hand away and gave a low whistle. "Wow, you sure do have some strong grip for such a frail-looking fella."

Liu looked straight into his face. "The Universe is filled with illusion, Gospodin Dallum. Which of us is ever really the person he appears to be?"

Jules stared at Liu. Through his mind raced the dozens of different — and sometimes contradictory — tales he'd heard about the mysterious Anarians and their even more mysterious powers of the mind. Was Liu telling him that he'd seen through Jules's disguise already? Could Liu be the assassin, playing word games to tease those around him? Could both of the questions be true? Or was Liu just playing the role of the Anarian mystic, making simple statements sound profound for theatrical effect?

There was no clue whatsoever in the other man's face. Those two dark eyes stared out at Jules impassively, without show of emotion. Whatever game Liu was playing, he was not about to tip his hand just yet.

Jules could not afford to tip his hand, either. He let John Dallum stare, amazed, at Liu for several seconds. "That sure is a deep thought," he said at last.

Liu bowed his head. "It's not original with me, I'm afraid. I'm just a humble scholar of philosophy."

"Say, I admire that. I've always wanted to be a philosopher myself, but I've always been too busy. We'll have to talk about it sometime."

"Indeed we will, Gospodin Dallum."

Jules walked away after Symond. "He's a strange one, isn't he?"

"Yes," Symond admitted. "None of us has been able to

get particularly close to him. But he's a polite enough chap, if a little distant."

Jules was trying to recall what he knew about Liu from the files. Anares did not keep very thorough records of its citizens, and Liu's file had been the sparsest of the lot. But Jules knew that Liu's claim to being a humble philosophy student was a mistruth. At the age of only twenty-eight, Choyen Liu was an ordained priest and was recognized as one of the top philosophical mystics on the entire planet of Anares.

"Certainly an unusual bunch of people, aren't we?" Jules said to his guide, and he meant it. Each young man present was the best his planet could produce . . . and yet, Jules had to contend with the possibility that one of them was a potential assassin. "Yes, sir, a real unusual bunch."

The Princess and her party, including Yvette, arrived two days later. When the two women had met again they had greeted each other as long lost sisters, despite the fact that they had met once before, for a single evening a year earlier. But a close bond had been cemented then, and the two resumed their relationship as though there had been no gap at all. They had much to tell each other on the long trip from Earth to Ansegria, and they spent the time almost constantly in each other's company.

Yvonne and Jacques Roumenier met them at the spaceport, having arrived from DesPlaines several hours earlier. Yvette introduced this other brother-sister team of DesPlainian agents to the Princess; the Roumeniers were suitably awed, but Edna quickly put them at their ease. Vonnie and Jacques were given uniforms indicating they were members of the Princess's official bodyguards, and were introduced to the rest of Her Highness's staff. That bit of business over with, the entire party proceeded to Rockhold Castle.

This time, the Baron and Baroness were on hand to greet her personally. The castle was decked out with banners and pennons, and the Imperial flag flew above the banner of Cambria on the staff. Amid a flourish of trumpets, the Princess was led through the gate into the courtyard to meet her old friends, the rulers of Cambria.

Baron Piers Howell was a tall man in his late fifties. His

39

face had aged with dignity, and no one could have imagined a more noble countenance. His hair was white, but his eyes held a spark of life that denied the years. His wife, the Baroness Ximena, was a petite woman several years his junior. She had an olive complexion and dark hair, and moved in quick, frenetic bursts of activity. She had a ready laugh and a charming manner that was legendary throughout the Sector.

This noble pair greeted the Princess warmly with kisses on the cheeks, then went on about the formal business of speechmaking. They said, in more words than it pays to recount, how pleased they were that she was honoring them with her presence and that they would do everything they could to make her stay enjoyable. Then the Princess, one lady-in-waiting (Yvette) and two bodyguards (Jacques and Yvonne), were escorted into the dining hall, while the rest of Her Highness's retinue busied themselves with transporting the Princess's numerous pieces of luggage into her prearranged quarters.

The candidates were already in the dining hall, and they naturally stood when the Imperial party entered the room. Yvette spotted her brother seated with the other candidates, but gave him no sign of recognition. Besides, she could tell that his eyes were busy elsewhere—Vonnie had entered the room, too.

It is much to the credit of those two young lovers that they did not show in their faces the emotions they felt in their hearts. They had not seen each other for several weeks and their longing to be together had grown considerably; but they knew that to betray those emotions would be to betray their mission for the Empire. So, with admirable willpower, they kept their eyes mostly to the fore, with only occasional glances in the other's direction.

Crown Princess Edna took her place at the head of the table, between the Baron and Baroness, but did not sit down immediately. Instead, she looked over the men assembled in front of her for a silent moment. Then she spoke.

"Dear friends, and those of you whom I hope to soon call friends. I know that this is a new and exciting experience for you, and that you may be a little nervous at meeting me. But I must point out that a Progress is no place for formality—it defeats the entire purpose. I will give you only two orders as your Princess. The first is that you are to treat me simply as Edna Stanley, a young lady about the same age as yourselves; the first one who calls me 'Your Imperial Highness' gets tossed in the pool by me personally." She paused to let that have effect. "The second order is: enjoy yourselves. Now, let's eat, I'm starving."

Jules and Yvette risked an exchange of glances as they sat down to supper. The same thought was uppermost in both their minds. The Progress had now begun. For the next two weeks, they and they alone were responsible for the safety of the heiress to the Empire.

And somewhere, a time bomb could be ticking.

Chapter 4

Evekian the Arranger

When the Circus of the Galaxy arrived at a new planet, it was no small event. Duke Etienne had several advance men out taking care of prepublicity. Advertisements normally were in all the newsrolls and broadcast over all the television, radio, and sensable networks at least a week in advance of the arrival, telling about the wonders and the marvels to be seen in the Galaxy's Greatest Show.

On Kolokov, of course, there had been little time for such advance publicity because of the suddenness of the Duke's decision to go there. That suddenness was not suspect, however, for Duke Etienne had something of a reputation for doing the unexpected—usually, though not always, at the whim of the Service of the Empire.

But even with just a few spot announcements scattered here and there, the Circus still attracted the public's attention. It had not played on this planet for nearly twenty years, and its reputation as the Galaxy's premiere entertainment event ensured massive popular interest.

As usual, a crowd gathered at the spaceport just to watch the crews unload. The Circus traveled about in twelve enormous cargo ships that carried all their paraphernalia, and these ships squatted at one end of the spaceport field while the equipment was loaded onto trucks to be carried to the fairgrounds where they would actually perform.

The d'Alemberts could not entrust the loading and unloading of their specialized equipment to the hands of regular dock workers; consequently, they did it all themselves. Everyone, from the star performers down to the behind-the-scenes work crews, pitched in and helped. But just because it was work did not mean it couldn't be fun as well.

The unloading was itself a show. The strongmen tossed enormous crates around as though they were loaded with feathers, making the onlookers gasp at their skills. The aerialists and acrobats bounced all over the scene, flying through the air with smaller boxes, arranging packages on the truck beds, fetching crates that appeared to be stored in places impossible for humans to reach without mechanical assistance. The clowns ran amok through the area, seeming to create endless chaos yet actually coordinating the whole event. The wild animals, when brought out in their cages, were suitably savage to chill and excite the most bored observer. There was music, noise, bright colors and chaos; yet despite all the apparent pandemonium, the unloading was done with unbelievable efficiency and in a minimum amount of time.

This performance was free to the thousands who thronged to the spaceport to watch it; but it was not wasted. For there was hardly a witness to it who did not then and there vow to go see the full Circus when it was finally set up and in operation. The unloading was just one more effective publicity stunt by the crafty Duke Etienne.

The actual setting up of the main tents and the midway was done in a more casual and relaxed manner since it was in the seclusion of the fairgrounds, where outsiders could be kept from seeing it until the Circus officially opened. Specialized crews took care of such details, while the performers rested up for their own tasks.

All was going smoothly in preparation for the show's opening the next day, but Etienne d'Alembert could not relax. Not only did he carry on his shoulders the massive responsibility of keeping all aspects of the Circus running without incident, but he also had the weightier task of coordinating the sub rosa activities for SOTE.

The Duke was a short man, as were most DesPlainians, standing but 160 centimeters tall. Though he himself had been a prime performer in his youth, he was inclining toward portliness more and more as middle age overtook him. His hair was thinning in front and graying at the temples, but his eyes normally had a humorous gleam to them. He looked so innocuous that he could have been mistaken for anyone's favorite uncle; but to evaluate him thusly would have been a grave error. For though his body was round, it was not soft—and behind that cheerful facade lay a mind that, in matters of espionage and intelligence, was second—perhaps—only to that of the Head of SOTE himself.

At present the Duke was conferring with his brother Marcel, the Circus's magician—and Etienne's partner in many daring exploits in their younger days. Marcel was tall and thin for a d'Alembert—at 180 centimeters and eighty kilograms, he was virtually a DesPlainian beanpole. "We have no specific orders, then?" Marcel asked in the French-English patois that was the native language of Des-Plaines.

"The Head left it entirely to our discretion," the Duke replied. "Our only instructions are to find out as much as possible about the bomb threat and to stop it at this end if we can. If not, we're to message Jules and Yvette on Ansegria so that they can take effective action there."

"And we have only one clue, this man called Winsted. So we must do some ferreting, *n'est-ce pas?*"

"*Oui.* I figured that the most logical approach was to check Winsted's roots, such as they were. He was, by occupation, closely associated with thieves of various sorts. This was not his native planet; he must have come here for some specific reason, probably related to the bomb threat. But that sort of man will seldom make a long journey just for one job, and I'm willing to bet he established contact with some other criminals just to 'make the trip worth it," as it were.

"The local SOTE office furnished me with a list of some of the better known contact points for the higher-class members of the underworld—the kind Winsted would be associating with. By mentioning his name around often enough, we should evoke enough interest to learn something from the reaction. After all, most of the underworld doesn't even know that Winsted was picked up yet—just that he's missing."

"When do we start?" Marcel asked, rubbing his hands together in anticipation.

"Ah, Marcel, always the eager one, eh? Well, it's possible we may get to see some action on this assignment, but not right now. There are others in our family who are equally qualified and who occasionally like a chance to have some of the fun. We mustn't be piggish about these things."

"Then who is handling it?"

"I've put Luise in charge. She can use the experience, and I think she'll do quite nicely."

Luise deForrest was the daughter of Emil deForrest and Etienne's and Marcel's sister Margaret. She was not as obviously DesPlainian as many other members of the d'Alembert family, being relatively tall and slender, which was one of the reasons why the Duke had chosen her for this assignment. At this early stage of the game there was no point to advertising the fact that DesPlainians were involved in this investigation—it would draw unwelcome suspicion onto the Circus.

Luise was not beautiful in the classical sense, but she had the strong presence of personality that many simply beautiful women lacked. Her thin face was highlighted by eyes that shone with intelligence, and she had a long, thin nose whose tip wiggled slightly when she spoke. Long black hair flowed elegantly down her back. Though she was only in her middle twenties, Luise was already one of the Circus's premiere clowns and mimes—and she possessed one of the sharpest young minds in the family. A natural clown had to be able to think quickly, and Luise was one of the best.

She was dressed in a loose-fitting blouse and long skirt that was the current fashion on the planet Belange, where Winsted had originally come from, and her shoulders were covered by a brown waist-length capelet. She walked in a brisk, businesslike manner, and the stern look in her eyes was that of a woman who brooked no nonsense from anyone.

Luise walked into Brovnik's Cocktail Lounge and went directly up to the bar. "A Starship Sling," she ordered. Though she shared, along with all DesPlainians, an allergy to alcohol, she *could* drink the stuff; the results would be uncomfortable for her metabolism, but a member of the Clan d'Alembert would do almost anything in the line of duty. As the bartender mixed the drink for her, Luise turned to survey the lounge.

The room was darkened to highlight the entertainment, which was a holographic recording of two female dancers doing an impressionistic performance of their art to Raussad's *Opus Number 4*. All around the stage were tables which were less than crowded—not unusual, considering this was a week night. A few other people stood around, either at the bar or a few meters away; several of them were engaged in private conversations, and the SOTE agent saw the flash of money being exchanged at one spot. She could not tell how much or what it was for.

Her drink arrived, and she took as small a sip as she could get away with while still appearing to enjoy it. "I'm looking for a friend of mine," she said conversationally to the bartender. "Perhaps you know him, he asked me to meet him here. His name's Rawl Winsted."

By the way the bartender's eyebrows arched quickly, Luise could tell that the man had heard that name before. The other recovered his demeanor, though; aside from that one little flick there was no sign of recognition. "No, can't say that I have. Of course, I see a lot of people go by here every day; maybe if you described him I could remember him better."

Luise pulled out a ten-ruble bill, folded it, and set it gently down on edge on top of the bar. She was very glad this bartender knew the victim; this was the eleventh spot she'd visited, and she was running low on bribe money. "Well, he's tall and kind of skinny, with long, delicate fingers—usually wears gloves, in fact. Dresses fairly conservatively. Dark, heavy eyebrows. . . ."

"Yeah, I think I know the guy you mean," the barkeep said, palming the bill with one deft gesture and putting it in his own pocket. "Came in here a couple of times with some friends."

"Do you know where I might find him or these friends?"

The bartender hesitated a second, then said, "Sure. Gospodin Cheevers over here was one of them." He signaled the indicated man to come over, and when he did the bartender continued, "Jos, this lady here is looking for Rawl Winsted."

The man called Jos Cheevers was big, nearly a full two meters tall and close to a hundred kilos in mass. His looming posture was carefully calculated to make smaller people feel ill-at-ease. "Yeah?" he said in a gravelly voice. "What's your business with Winsted?"

"He sent for me," Luise said calmly.

Cheevers's eyes narrowed. "You his woman or somethin'?"

Luise's glare would have pierced a hole through a bar of iron. "I'm his partner. We worked together back on Belange. He sent me a message a couple of weeks ago that he wanted to see me here, that he might have some work for me."

"What kind of work do you do?"

"The same kind Rawl does."

The big man looked at her curiously. "What did Winsted tell you about his job here?"

"I believe," Luise said slowly, "I have told you all I am going to, for the present. Perhaps if you would tell me where I can find Rawl, you and I could talk further."

Cheevers was not used to having a woman speak to him in such a manner. In the social circles he frequented, there were only two types of females: the shy, decent ones whom he could terrify and bully, and the brash, indecent ones who would accept anything he had to say with bland passivity. This woman did not fit into either category, and that disturbed him. "What's your name?"

Luise deForrest just looked at him, not saying a word. Cheevers stood beside her for a moment, just clenching and unclenching his fists, then finally said, "Wait here. I gotta make a call."

Luise watched patiently as the big man went over to the booth and placed a communicator call to someone whose face Luise could not make out over the vision screen. The agent dared not crane her neck or appear anxious. All she could do was wait until Cheevers had finished his call, sipping slowly on her drink and trying not to wince as the alcohol burned its way down her throat.

The big man came back from the com booth and stood beside her. "Come along with me," he ordered.

"Will you take me to Rawl?"

"Yeah."

Since Luise knew that Winsted was dead, she doubted the big man's sincerity. "I haven't finished my drink yet."

"I thought you wanted to meet your friend."

47

"What proof do I have that you'll really take me to him?"

Cheevers moved up closely against her and nudged her in the side. Luise could feel the hard, circular rim of a weapon pressing into her ribs. She couldn't tell whether it was a blaster or merely a stun-gun, but she didn't particularly want to take chances with either. "This is my proof," Cheevers growled.

"Ah, well, as long as you put it that way, of course," Luise replied. "I never argue with irrefutable evidence." She set the drink down on the bar—with inward thanks at not having to drink the rest of it—and moved toward the door with Cheevers directly behind her.

Another man joined them at the door. The newcomer was only slightly smaller than Cheevers but looked, if anything, tougher. Together, the two men escorted Luise out the door and into the darkness of the night. *Wherever they're taking me,* the agent thought, *they certainly want to make sure I get there.* "Why couldn't Rawl come and meet me himself?" she asked aloud.

"Shut up," was Cheever's laconic reply.

"Is he in any danger? Is he hiding out? You can tell me, I'm his partner."

"I said, shut up!" Cheevers raised his hand as though to smack the woman across the face—but he did not carry through on that action for one very good reason. The reason's name was Richard d'Alembert.

Rick, as he was known to his family and friends, was the leader of the Circus's team of wrestlers. As such, he was better than a hundred kilos of the most efficient fighting machine capable of being packaged in a body of flesh and bone. Not only were his muscles supertightened for action, but he had training in every branch of the martial arts and the speed to carry out his actions before most ordinary opponents would be able to think straight.

He had come along with Luise and waited outside the lounge just in case some trouble might arise. Luise's situation was obvious as soon as she emerged with the two toughs, and Rick had followed them along in the shadows until the moment came for him to make his move.

That moment was now, with Cheevers's arm raised to attack in a different direction and the other blasterbat's

48

attention focused on his comrade. Rick launched himself at Cheevers with all the strength in his massive Des-Plainian body.

Cheevers, caught by surprise, fell forward as Rick's body hit him from the rear. The Circus wrestler came down on top of his foe, landing a succession of blows to the body designed to daze any opponent. Cheevers, a veteran of many tough fights, was a little more resilient than an ordinary person, and did manage to attempt one blow back at his assailant. Rick parried that swing easily with his forearm, then returned it with a vengeance. His fist caught Cheevers squarely on the jaw, knocking the thug's head back against the sidewalk. Cheevers went out like a light.

Meanwhile, Luise had not been inactive. Clowns, as well as athletes, had to keep themselves in top physical condition to perform their acts, and members of the Family d'Alembert were more than ordinarily rigorous in their training. She knew that Rick was waiting for the opportunity to attack, and was not caught by surprise when her relative did so. As Rick came flying at Cheevers, Luise stepped aside so that the two bodies fell past her to the ground. At the same time, she turned to the other crook and brought her foot down squarely on the man's instep. The thug howled with pain, but the yell was cut short as Luise swung her fist, with all the not inconsiderable DesPlainian strength at her disposal, into the pit of her opponent's stomach.

There was a *whoosh* of air as the man doubled over. Luise interlaced her fingers, thereby locking her hands into one powerful unit, and brought it down on the top of her foe's exposed head. There was a dull *thunk* as she connected solidly; then the man fell to the ground and lay quite still.

Luise clapped her hands together as though brushing off some imaginary dirt and looked over at Rick. The wrestler was just getting to his feet, a big grin on his face. "For someone who makes a living at being funny," he said jovially, "you sure taught that bruiser a serious lesson."

"Thank you, cousin," Luise said with a mock curtsy. "Your timing was pretty good, too. But I think we should stop congratulating each other and take care of our two

49

friends here. Cheevers, the one you knocked out, shouldn't be under too long—at least, I hope not."

"I gave him but the gentlest of taps," Rick assured her.

"Good, because we have to learn where he was taking me—and fast. If we're not there in a reasonable time, Cheevers's boss might get a little suspicious and that would only make our job harder."

Together, they dragged the two men back to their waiting car. The second thug was tied and gagged securely and stashed away in the back seat. Cheevers also was bound, but they made no attempt to cover his mouth — they wanted him to talk. Then they revived him and began their questioning.

Their methods of interrogation were less than polite, but about on a par with what Cheevers would have used had the roles been reversed. Thus, in a surprisingly short time they learned that Cheevers had been ordered by his boss—a man named Evekian—to bring the mysterious woman to his office immediately for further inquiry. Coercion was authorized if the victim did not want to come voluntarily. The d'Alemberts also learned the location of Evekian's headquarters and the details of how the place was guarded. By the time he was finished telling them what he knew, Cheevers was barely conscious; the two agents left him tied up in the back seat and placed a coded call back to the Circus.

A team of their relatives was all set, just awaiting the word from them to move into action. Luise gave the address of the headquarters and described a preliminary plan of attack. She was told that the assault group would meet her there in fifteen minutes.

As scheduled, the d'Alemberts rendezvoused in the darkness outside the headquarters building. The ground level of this block was mostly stores and commercial establishments, but the top five floors of this one building were staffed by Evekian and his minions. Evekian himself lived on the fourth floor, with several floors standing between himself and an invasion from any ground forces, plus one floor of defense above him in case enemies (or the police) should land by copter on the roof. The only way out onto the street was down a narrow flight of stairs that led out of a currently locked door. Cheevers had said there would be a pair of guards at the top of those steps, and that both would be armed with blasters.

A setup like that would have daunted many people, but the Family d'Alembert was quite adept at performing the impossible. Frontal attacks from the stairs or from the roof would have resulted in Pyrrhic victories at best; they chose to go around the trouble and sneak up behind it.

Among the attacking force was a goodly percentage of acrobats and aerialists. They thought nothing, even in the darkness of Kolokov's night, of scaling the walls of the building on the outside, using grappling hooks, ropes, and pulleys to lift themselves to positions outside the windows facing the street. All of them were armed with stun-guns—and, more importantly, their own unique talents as rough-and-tumble fighters.

On a given signal, they launched their attack simultaneously from several spots at once. Kicking in the glass of the windows, they crashed into the rooms beyond, tumbled, and kept on running. This first wave had their stunners at the ready and set on four—a two-hour stun. Anything that moved—anything that even looked like it *might* move—was given a dose of stun rays from the d'Alemberts' guns.

This first wave of assault encountered no resistance. The defenders were caught flatfooted; if there was any trouble expected at all, it was supposed to have been from one woman whom Cheevers had picked up in a bar—not from an army of expertly trained agents. Not a single shot was fired in defense as those people still in the building at this hour fell from the d'Alembert assault.

But, quick as the d'Alemberts were, they were not quite fast enough to stop an alarm from being raised. The noise of the shattering glass windows alone would have alerted the forces inside; that and the fact that several of the people had time to push alarm buzzers before they were felled meant that the d'Alemberts had won only the preliminary skirmish. The full battle royal lay ahead.

More and more d'Alemberts poured in through the windows as the shock troops pressed onward. The corridors outside the offices became battlefields, with the buzzing of stun-guns reaching an almost monotonous staccato. Plenty of the defenders slumped to the ground

51

under the relentless assault, but there were also a large number of d'Alemberts among the bodies that were soon littering the halls. The DesPlainians were stronger, quicker, and better trained than the people they were fighting, but they were not perfect.

Within two minutes, though, the objective of this first wave was achieved—the two guards at the top of the front stairs had been eliminated. That left the way open for Rick's team of wrestlers—not quite as adept at climbing the ropes to the upper stories as their relatives—to come storming into the fray. These were the real troops, each better than 110 kilograms of calculated mayhem. What they couldn't shoot, they simply battered their way through, berserking in combat like a horde of barbarians. Their hoarse battlecries alone struck terror into the hearts of the building's defenders, and the sight of those moving mountains of humanity was enough to dismay even the most stalwart crook. Most of Evekian's guards were so stunned by the thought of Rick's men charging down on top of them that they forgot to even fire their weapons. The d'Alemberts moved triumphantly through the halls and upward to the third floor.

It was at this level that they encountered blaster fire, and they had to proceed a little more cautiously. Once again the acrobats were brought in, for the speed of their reflexes was greater, if only by an instant, than those of the wrestlers. These people could roll into the corridor so quickly that the defenders would have trouble taking aim; the first shots fired usually missed, but it gave the acrobats a chance to spot where their enemies were. The d'Alemberts' first shots were usually much more accurate. Then the acrobats would roll behind some cover and wait for the opportunity to pull the trick again.

Slowly but surely they gained ground until finally the third floor was theirs. Quickly the wrestling team moved on up to the largely undefended fourth floor where Evekian lived. They found it empty.

The crime boss, after waiting a minute to see how the battle was progressing, realized that his forces were being overwhelmed. He was not one to go down with his ship, so, since there was no indication of activity on the roof, he headed up in that direction to his own personal copter. Once there, he figured to escape easily.

He had just seated himself at the controls, though, when a female voice spoke up calmly behind him. "Easy there, *Tovarishch*. I've got a stunner here, and I've got no compunctions against using it." At the same time, Evekian could feel the hard plastic nozzle press against the back of his head, so that he would know the threat was not an idle one.

Luise deForrest moved from the back of the cockpit over to the seat beside the pilot's, her aim never wavering from Evekian's head. The criminal leader, being both a realist and a coward, made no attempt to escape. "I don't know who you are or why your people are attacking my offices," he said, "but you've obviously made some mistake."

"The mistake, *mon ami*, is yours, for siccing Cheevers on me in the first place. But I'm going to let you rectify it. The two of us are going to have a nice long talk about a certain Rawl Winsted and why he came to Kolokov."

"Evekian was really rather helpful once I persuaded him to start talking," Luise reported to the Duke several hours later. "He didn't want to say anything at first—kept insisting I was mistaking him for someone else. As though anyone without something to hide would keep his offices staffed with an army like that. But eventually Rick and I induced him to part with the information we wanted. I think it was the threat to make him a soprano in the choir that did it."

Duke Etienne leaned back in his chair and stifled a yawn. It was very early in the morning and he had stayed up all night awaiting Luise's report. He wished she would get to the point, but he knew from long experience the futility of rushing his niece when she was relating a story.

"It turns out," Luise continued, unaware of the Duke's restiveness, "that this Evekian is a big arranger here on Kolokov. He doesn't necessarily do very much himself, but he arranges things for other people—for a commission. If you knew the inside setup for a robbery, for instance, but didn't have the necessary skills to carry off the job, you would contact Evekian and he'd find you just the man to help. If you needed a murder committed, he'd find the killer and you would have an airtight alibi. He's sort of like a marriage broker, getting rich off of other people's talents and abilities.

"In the case of Rawl Winsted, he'd been asked to find an expert in dealing with miniature workings like watches. There are plenty of legitimate jewelers around, but the client specified someone with a background of illegality and who didn't have a scruple to his name. Evekian sent for Winsted. Part of the job specification was that Winsted would have to agree to have the hypnotic block implanted; but he was getting paid so much money for the job that a slight loss of his memory wasn't so terrible a price to pay in return."

"Does Evekian know what the job was?"

Luise shook her head. "He says he doesn't, and I tend to believe him. Evekian's the sort who wouldn't ask, on the theory that he's not an accessory to the crime if he doesn't know what the crime is. But Winsted performed his function, was paid, and then disappeared. Evekian thought that would be the end of it, until I showed up, claiming to be Winsted's partner whom he'd sent for to help him work on this job. Naturally Evekian didn't want anyone coming into the picture unless he got his commission on it, so he had me picked up to 'discuss' the matter with me. It didn't work out that way."

"Did you at least find out the name of the client who wanted Winsted's services?"

Luise drew in a deep breath. "Yes, I did. It was Fyodor Paskoi—Duke of Kolokov."

Chapter 5

Competitions

The Princess's Progress started out in a relaxed enough way with a ride down the beach. Everyone in the Princess's party was given a dorvat, a hexapedal animal about the size of a burro. They were native to Ansegria, and had proved easily tamable for riding. It took a little while for non-Ansegrians to get used to the strange six-legged gait of these creatures, and a good deal of fun was had at the expense of those members of the party who were particularly less adept at dealing with the tranquil but clumsy beasts. Jules especially made himself look less agile than he was, and had a lot of fun poked at him—all of which he took in good-natured stride, as befitted the character of John Dallum.

The Princess's retinue had been carefully balanced so that there were enough ladies-in-waiting to complement the candidates. Thus, no one would be without companionship of a member of the opposite sex during any of the events scheduled for the coming two weeks, and it was Edna's duty to mingle among the men and try to spend as much time with each of them as she could. In this way, she hoped to find her future consort and the father of the next Stanley ruler after herself.

The day was sunny and warm; the weather was nearly always pleasant around Cambria, especially at this time of the year. As the party rode their dorvats along the oceanside, the Princess chatted with one young man named Hans Gudding. He was a banker's son from the planet

Vandergast, and was making quite a name for himself in the world of interstellar finance—particularly dealing in agricultural futures. He explained to her the problems of that trade: how he had to keep apprised of the total food situation on not just one but several planets; how he had to spot the trends developing at least two years in advance; how he had to buy as discreetly as possible, since too much activity in one area could affect the outcome adversely; and how he had to keep updating his figures and weeding out the bad investments while continuing to improve his stock on hand.

The subject was not as dry as it sounds, because Hans Gudding was a very personable young man with a great deal of enthusiasm for his subject, and such enthusiasm is generally contagious. Edna listened with interest that was unfeigned; she'd had a considerable amount of training about the ins and outs of finance on interstellar levels, and knew that she would need even more knowledge about such intricate matters once she assumed the Throne. The ruler of this vast galactic empire had to know a great deal about nearly every subject known to man, and Edna still considered herself woefully ignorant of entirely too much.

So she listened intently as the young man spoke, occasionally interjecting a question or comment of her own. She fielded very expertly his not-so-subtle hints that she should choose a husband who was as adept as he was at manipulating situations and dealing with people. She had been on enough previous Progresses to know that she was not really a person to most of these men, but merely an object that could bring them untold wealth and power. It was one of the facets of these jaunts that dismayed her the most, and turned what should be pleasant vacations into boring duties.

They arrived at a predetermined spot on the beach where the Baron's servants had gone ahead and prepared a barbecue lunch for the party. There was talking and laughing on the sand as they ate, and Edna took the opportunity to slip politely away from Gospodin Gudding and mingle with some of the other young men available.

After lunch, Anton Borov suggested some competitions as a method of passing the time. Jules suspected that he had made the suggestion because he expected to win and therefore bring himself more to the Princess's notice. At any rate, the idea met with general approval, and they bickered for a while over what forms those contests would take. Some wrestling matches were agreed on first, after which there were to be some races. Most of the men were eager to participate, with the exception of Choyen Liu, who sat silently off to one side while the others were limbering up. Curious, Edna went over to him. "Aren't you going to compete?" she asked him.

"No," he said. "To compete is to acknowledge the illusion of life that some arbitrary goals are more important than inward revelation. I prefer to let the others do the competing, if they must."

"You don't believe in competing, yet you're along on this Progress, competing for my hand. Doesn't that strike you as contradictory?"

"Not at all. You are a creature with free will, as are we all. You will eventually make your choice; I was chosen by my planet as one of your alternatives, nothing more. To strive against the other men would be folly, because you would still have to consider their virtues and faults. Only by killing all of them, and thus depriving you of alternatives, would competition avail me."

The novelty of Liu's ideas was so unexpected that Edna could just stare at him, stunned. *What an odd young man,* she thought. His objectivity was refreshing after so many clamors for her attentions. *I should learn more about him. After all, the planet Anares will be part of my realm, and I should learn how the people think and act, and what they want and need.* But despite her interest, and despite the fact that she was normally a well-spoken young lady, she could think of nothing further to say to this stranger. He seemed to transcend the normal topics of conversation. So, instead, she sat silently by his side and watched the action taking place on the beach before her.

The wrestling matches quickly showed that they were a contest between three people—Jules, Paul Symond, and Anton Borov. Jules knew that, with his incredible DesPlainian strength and physical training, he could best either of the other two; but he also knew that to do so would be to blow his cover identity. So, in the semi-final match, he lost gracefully to Symond and sat back on the sand to watch the outcome of the final pairing.

It was a hard-fought battle. It was clear to Jules quite

early that Symond was the better fighter, being both stronger and more agile. Borov, though, was much more determined to win. As he and Symond circled one another there was an expression of near-animal ferocity on the face of the Kolokovnik. He attacked again and again with blows that were far too savage for friendly competition, and only Symond's agility enabled him to escape without injury. Then Borov finally managed to flip his opponent onto the ground and came down hard on top of him. The Lateestan wriggled like an eel and finally managed to twist out of the other's grasp, turning him over and pinning him to the ground instead. Borov had to concede the match.

The next competition was to be foot races along the shore, but that idea turned out to be impractical; the sand was so loose that it was difficult to gain solid footing except right down at the waterline. Borov came up with an alternative suggestion: "Why don't we race on our dorvats?"

"Will they run?" another of the men asked dubiously. "They seem so tranquil."

"Of course they will," Borov said. "All animals that can walk can run; how else can they escape from predators and from fires? It's just a question of giving them the proper motivation. Who's game?"

Five of the other candidates, including Symond, decided to take up Borov's challenge. Jules decided to sit out this particular contest. He was not as confident of his abilities with an unpredictable animal—particularly with a species unfamiliar to him. Forcing a strange beast to do something it was not trained for could have dire consequences.

The half dozen contestants lined their mounts up in a line at one spot along the beach. They were to race to a rock about a kilometer down the shore, then turn their mounts around and race back to the starting point.

At the starting signal, all six men dug their heels into the flanks of their dorvats. The animals, not trained for anything more than a gentle, loping gait, did not react to this at first, so several of the men dug in harder. The dorvats panicked and began rearing; the riders, not expecting this maneuver, were thrown from their saddles to the ground. The panic was contagious, and all six of the animals were trampling about and threatening to grind the men beneath their hooves.

Jules, Jacques, and Yvonne reacted instantly to the

menace by running to the scene and trying to help. Yvette thought of going with them, then decided against it; *someone* had to stay by Edna's side, no matter what, in case this miniature stampede were only a diversion to attract people's attention while the threatened time bomb was planted. While everyone else's eyes were on the scene below, hers were on everyone else. But she saw no suspicious activity.

The trio of DesPlainians reached the site of the action just seconds after the riders were thrown, due to the quickness of their reflexes and their fantastic speed. All at once they found themselves in the middle of a forest of flailing legs. The dorvats had six limbs apiece, and each animal massed better than three hundred kilograms—a formidable obstacle to face. Dodging under the flying hooves, Jules reached for one of the fallen bodies. The man, a Nagalian named Itsu Yabashi, had been stunned by his fall to the earth, and would have been helpless under the dorvats' feet. Jules pulled him to safety, noticing that Yvonne and Jacques were similarly occupied rescuing others of the candidates. Symond, Jules noted happily, had managed to retain his senses and crawl away from the area of danger. He was now standing to one side, not sure precisely what to do and thus being of no positive help. But he was one less body the DesPlainians would have to remove.

Jules spotted Anton Borov lying prone directly in the center of the stampede. Hooves and rearing dorvat bodies were scattered all around him. Dodging between the frightened animals, he tried to make it to Borov's side.

The middle left hoof of one dorvat caught him on the side of the head. Though it was barely a glancing blow, the creature's three-hundred-kilo mass gave it a lot of impact. Jules staggered slightly to the side, and collided with the body of another dorvat. This second encounter knocked him to the ground, right into the path of a third oncoming dorvat.

Vonnie, his fiancée, saw what had happened and gave an involuntary shriek. In an instant she had dropped the body she was carrying and had started in Jules's direction to save him. Her brother Jacques, who had not been watching Jules, looked up as she cried out, and sized up the situation at a glance. He, too, dropped his burden and started into the melee to rescue his future brother-in-law.

But both of them knew they would not be in time. They were on the other side of the group, and had too much distance to cover, dodging through the panic-stricken dorvats, to reach Jules before the danger did.

As Jules tried his best to roll out of the way of the charging beast, he felt the presence of another person in the area. Out of the corner of his eye, he could see the slim, slight form of Choyen Liu racing into the fray. One part of his mind had the fraction of a second it needed to wonder what this fragile-looking religious scholar hoped to achieve with this act of bravery.

Then the Anarian was beside the raging steed, seemingly unfazed by its flailing hooves. Reaching up with one hand, he began stroking the creature's short, stubby neck and making trilling sounds to soothe its confused mind. The dorvat slowed its charge and began to return to its more tranquil self, and this slight slowing was all Jules needed. He rolled free of the oncoming animal's path. By that time, Vonnie had reached him and was helping him to his feet, and together the two of them left the danger zone. Jacques Roumenier finished Jules's task of rescuing Borov.

Yvonne's first impulse once she and Jules were out of peril was to smother him with kisses and tell him how happy she was that he was all right. But her sharp agent's instincts came to the fore and reminded her that she and Jules were still acting the parts of total strangers. Restraining herself admirably, she looked him over with a formal glance and said, "Are you hurt, Gospodin?"

"All smooth," Jules replied, winking back at her. Then he turned to see what was happening with the panicked dorvats.

Choyen Liu was doing a remarkable job. Without any trace of fear he walked calmly through the crowd of frightened beasts talking to them, trilling at them, touching them gently, and in general soothing the confusion and pain in their meager minds. Although the animals were still reacting wildly when he entered the area, he moved among them without being touched and, within thirty seconds, had calmed them down to an approachable level; and, while they were still snorting uneasily, they were no longer a threat.

Jules was frankly astonished. He had only seen one other

person who could handle animals that well—his second-cousin Jeanne d'Alembert who, at only seventeen, was the Circus's premiere animal trainer and was considered the top handler in the Galaxy. She had such an affinity with all living things that she could persuade the fiercest beasts man had found in the Galaxy to do her bidding. And it appeared that Choyen Liu had some of this talent, too. It was a fact to remember, and Jules stored the item in a corner of his mind.

For now, he simply got to his feet, walked over to the Anarian and patted him on the back. "Thank you," he said. "That was pretty fancy work you did there, saving my life."

"You showed a good deal of bravery yourself, risking your life to save several others," Liu countered. "If I may be permitted to say so, you look as though you were born to be a hero."

Again Liu was dropping hints that he thought Jules might be more than he seemed. And again Jules deliberately ignored the bait. "Come on," he said, "let's see if our comrades need any help."

By now everyone in the party was approaching the scene of the near-tragedy. The Princess's natural instincts had been to run over to the site once the danger from the dorvats was over, but Yvette reminded her that she was in enough peril already and that she should, for safety's sake, hang back a little. Consequently, while the rest of the group ran over to help, Edna, Yvette, and the rest of the bodyguards stayed at the top of a little hillock and watched what was going on.

All things considered, the injuries were very slight. One of the young men remained unconscious, though his breathing was regular and there was no sign of bleeding. Another of the candidates had twisted an ankle and had two fingers trod upon by a dorvat; otherwise he was all right. Borov regained consciousness and complained about sharp pains on the right side of his chest. Jules and several of the other people suspected he may have had a few ribs broken. One of the Princess's bodyguards was dispatched back to the castle with the news of what had happened, and shortly thereafter an ambulance copter arrived to take the injured men away.

The remaining members of the party rode their now

tranquil mounts back to Rockhold in gloomy silence. A pall had fallen over their spirits. This Progress, which was supposed to be such a pleasant experience for all concerned, had in its first day turned out to be a lot more serious a matter than most of the people had counted on.

Once back at the castle, there was a two-hour rest period to freshen up before dinner, during which time they learned the fate of the three injured members of their party. The young man who had remained unconscious had a concussion and a skull fracture; he would not be returning to the Progress. The one with the twisted ankle and the smashed fingers would be returning, though of necessity his physical activities would be limited. The doctors diagnosed three cracked ribs on Borov and wanted to keep him hospitalized for a while, but he insisted that he would be all right and asked to be allowed to return to the Progress. So, reluctantly, they taped up his ribcage, shot him full of regeneratives, and said they would send him back to Rockhold in the morning after one night in the hospital for observation.

With the knowledge of what had befallen their companions, the spirits of the group raised slightly. Making a monumental effort to shake off the afternoon's gloom, everyone came down to supper in their finest clothing and seemed determined to be carefree despite the incident. Edna ended up seated next to Paul Symond, and that young man proved to be a very agreeable dinner partner. He did not bore her ear off with talk about his job or about his qualifications to be her husband; instead, the two of them swapped incidents that had happened in their childhood, traded a couple of shaggy dog stories, and discussed items of current events in the newsrolls. By the time the meal was finished and she was to retire for the evening, the Princess had almost forgotten the unpleasantness of the afternoon.

She dismissed her maidservants and summoned Yvette to come alone into her room. "Well," she asked her friend and protector, "the Progress is now one day old. What do you think?"

"That's hard to say. I take it such excitement is not exactly common at these affairs."

"Hardly. This is the first time anything like that has happened. If it weren't for the fact that three people were hurt and more could have been, I would almost have welcomed the episode as a break in the monotony. But I was asking your professional opinion, primarily; how do things look with regard to your assignment?"

Yvette sighed. "I haven't spotted anything yet. I've been over your room thoroughly with the equipment the Head gave me; there aren't any bombs in here yet. I was planning to go over most of this wing of the castle once everyone's asleep, but it's an almost impossible job—bombs can be made so small these days. Our best hope is still to catch whoever's going to plant the bomb—if, indeed, there's going to be one."

"Any suspects?"

"I haven't had much time to look them over. I got a few minutes alone with Jules this afternoon to compare notes, but he's a little puzzled, too. All of them are theoretically loyal, yet all of them are potential assassins. Jules thought Borov should be the prime suspect, since he comes from Kolokov, the planet where Winsted was captured and where the plot apparently was conceived. I don't really like him too much."

Edna nodded in agreement. "Same here. He's far too intense, far too cocky. I've encountered that type before on these outings. He thinks pure brashness and snobbishness will get my attention, and he tries to show off at every opportunity. Marriage to him would be intolerable; he'd always consider himself right and he'd try to boss me around. I will want a partner to help me rule the Empire, but I can't tolerate a boss."

"He certainly is determined, though, insisting on staying with the Progress despite those broken ribs," Yvette mused. "I'm wondering whether it's because he's got an assignment to plant a bomb and doesn't want to leave until he's completed it." She shrugged. "Oh, well, Jules said he would go through Borov's room while he's still in the hospital and check for any traces of a bomb. If it's there, he'll find it.

"Jules also said he's keeping an eye on that Anarian, Choyen Liu. He said the man made some remark or other that made him a little suspicious."

"Choyen Liu is a very strange man," Edna agreed. "I talked to him a little bit this afternoon. I don't know what to make of him, he's so different from any other

63

man I've ever met. It would be so easy to just dismiss him as a mystic or a spouter of pontifical sayings, but then he does something like quieting those dorvats and you begin to wonder. He's certainly handsome, in an exotic sort of way. What do you think?"

"Can't say, I haven't really had any contact with him yet. But if Jules considers him a suspect, I'll keep an eye on him as well."

"And what do you think of Paul Symond?" Edna asked suddenly.

"As a potential assassin or as a potential Imperial Consort?"

"Both."

"As a suspect, he ranks equal with everyone else. As a man—" she grinned,—"I'd say *yummy*. As long as he's a ladykiller only in the metaphorical sense I'll have to restrain myself from slobbering all over his shoes. Can I have the leftovers when you're through with him?"

"I promise," Edna laughed. "That's the word of a princess. Yes, I was impressed with him, too. He's not so interested in proving he'd make a good Consort as in proving he'd make a good husband. That's mostly what I'm looking for." Her laughter faded into a warm smile and she looked straight into Yvette's eyes. "I'm so glad you're along, and not just as protection. You're a friend I can talk to, and we're about the same age. I need someone like that." She hugged Yvette, and the SOTE agent returned the gesture affectionately.

The two women talked some more, then Yvette left to prepare for her midnight rounds. Edna watched the door close behind her with satisfaction. With people like Jules and Yvette d'Alembert looking out for her welfare, she knew she would be able to sleep safely—tonight and every night.

Chapter 6

Invitation to Rimskor

On any planet where the Circus of the Galaxy played, Duke Etienne always made it a point to send free courtesy passes to all the local nobility, from the Baron in whose city the Circus was stationed all the way up to the Duke of the entire world. If Kolokov was any exception to this rule at all, it was because of the special attention Etienne d'Alembert paid to the invitation he sent Duke Fyodor Paskoi.

The invitation was handwritten in letters of pure gold and elaborately illuminated by Etienne's niece, Françoise, an expert in the almost extinct art of calligraphy. Included with this impressive-looking document was a note from Duke Etienne, extending his personal invitation as one duke to another to join him in his private box for a showing of the Galaxy's greatest performers, and to sample Duke Etienne's fabulous supply of wines and enjoy the cooking of his chefs, who were famed throughout the Galaxy.

The Duke was going to this trouble for a very special reason. It would be possible, of course, for him to order an assault team of his own into Duke Fyodor's stronghold; but such an endeavor would have been foolhardy. They would have no idea of the layout of the castle; no idea of the defenses they would be going up against; and, worst of all, no idea of what they were looking for. Three of his family had died in the assault on Evekian's offices, and another thirteen had been hospitalized. That operation would look like child's play compared to the losses he would sustain attacking a ducal fortress. He had no doubt he would win; he had supreme confidence in the abilities of his family, the most well-trained group of people in the history of the human race. But he wanted to bring the cost of the operation, in terms of lives, down to absolute minimal limits.

So instead, he was hoping to win his way into Duke Fyodor's favor and possibly receive an invitation in return to visit the local duke at his castle. Once inside, he would be able to size up the situation a little better and plan his attack from there.

He had, of course, considered the possibility of having the local SOTE office arrest the Duke just on the basis of what evidence they had obtained from Evekian, who was now being detained indefinitely. But there simply was not enough proof to act on. Dukes were of the second highest rank in the Empire's system of nobility, and questioning them was not as freewheeling an affair as questioning some minor criminal. As the Emperor's right arm, the Service of the Empire did have wide authority—but along with that authority came the responsibility not to abuse it. If Duke Fyodor did not voluntarily cooperate with his questioners, he would have to be held for a High Court of Justice to try his case—which could take months. In the meantime, the Crown Princess's life would still be in danger from the bomb threat. More subtle methods would have to be employed.

The reply from Duke Fyodor's social secretary was disappointing. The Duke, it was explained, seldom left his castle because of physical infirmities, and, in any event, could not indulge in rich foods or wines because his delicate system would not tolerate them. The Duke would be delighted to see the show via television hookup—his body would not tolerate sensable shows, either—if that would be agreeable to Duke Etienne.

The senior d'Alembert answered back promptly saying that he respected the fact of Duke Fyodor's health difficulties, but that it was against a nearly two-centuries old tradition of the Circus to broadcast their performances in any way. That was how they maintained such an interest in their show. He regretted that Duke Fyodor would be unable to share the food and drinks, but he reiterated that the

Circus was quite used to caring for people with many problems, and that the utmost attention would be paid to His Grace's particular needs. Duke Fyodor would be as well taken care of as if he were still in his own castle.

This time, the missive met with success. A letter came back saying that the Duke was pleased with Duke Etienne's concern, and would indeed be honored to be his guest at a performance of the Circus. A date was arranged for that very night, and Etienne was delighted. The Circus's manager began setting the wheels of his scheme in motion.

Duke Fyodor arrived in his own personal copter, accompanied by a smaller man whom he introduced as his physician, Dr. Immanuel Rustin. The sight of Duke Fyodor's skeletal figure, locked rigidly into its maze of tubing and machinery, startled Etienne at first, even though it had been described in SOTE's files on the man. He tried gamely not to react to the taut-stretched skin, bug eyes, and shining metal teeth, but apparently was not completely successful. Duke Fyodor smiled a death's head smile and said, "Yes, I have that effect on nearly everyone." His voice, coming from twin speakers on either side of his head, had an eerie effect.

"I meant no disrespect, Sir," Etienne answered at once. "I admit to being startled, but that's all. I'm dependent on prosthetics myself, you know."

To illustrate his point, Etienne held up his right arm and unscrewed the hand at the wrist. He had lost that member fourteen years ago to a stray blaster beam while on an assignment. The artificial hand that had replaced it was perfectly adequate for the job, as it was indistinguishable from a natural one; it was, in fact, more than adequate, because each of the fingers housed equipment of a very specialized nature. The fingers were detachable just above the knuckles, and Duke Etienne had different ones for different purposes; but this fact was not generally known outside the family. Etienne concealed the finger joinings with a series of gaudy rings.

Duke Fyodor's eyes lit up as he recognized another rebuilt human. "How did it happen?" he asked.

Etienne shrugged his shoulders. "Accidents will happen at times in a circus," he replied evasively.

As Duke Fyodor leaned forward to examine the false hand, Etienne noticed the odd piece of jewelry around the other's neck—an integrated circuit chip on a golden chain. *I've seen something like that once before,* he thought, but a quick skim of his memory failed to turn up a concrete image. Finally he gave up the effort for now, and relegated it to the status of an interesting datum. There were more important matters to attend to.

Now that the initial awkwardness had been cleared away, the two dukes got on quite nicely. As Etienne had promised, they had the best seats in the house, the manager's private box; and the performers, knowing that a very special guest was in the audience, put on an especially impressive display of their considerable talents. Duke Fyodor was flabbergasted by their acts.

"I must admit I've always admired good performances of physical agility. Perhaps it's because I've always been so limited in that direction myself, but I get a thrill out of watching people utilizing their bodies to perfection."

And when the show was over, Duke Fyodor told Duke Etienne how glad he was that he'd chosen to come, after all, and that he couldn't recall when he'd enjoyed himself more. "You really must be my guest while you're here on Kolokov. I know. I'm giving a diplomatic reception tomorrow evening for the ambassador from Horatia—it's the two hundred and fiftieth anniversary of the settling of their planet, and I have a big party planned. I insist that you come along as my guest, in return for your splendid hospitality today."

"I'd be delighted to come. May I bring my brother Marcel?"

"Of course. I absolutely adored his act. Do you think I could prevail upon him to perform for my guests tomorrow?"

Etienne d'Alembert smiled. He'd been hoping for just such an opportunity. "Yes, I know he'd be honored. Until tomorrow night, then." And the two dukes—one a traitor, the other a loyal agent of the Crown—parted amiably.

Duke Fyodor sent one of his personal limousines around to the Circus the next evening to pick up his two special guests. Duke Etienne d'Alembert of DesPlaines and Lord Marcel d'Alembert, to use their full titles, were dressed in all their formal splendor. The Duke was wearing a tunic of gray velvet over a pair of gray flared slacks. The tunic's sleeves were slashed to show the silver undersleeves beneath them. An unadorned platinum fillet rested on his head, almost hidden by the curls of his silver-gray hair, and a platinum chain hung down from his shoulders, supporting a single sapphire in the center of his chest that matched the sapphires in the rings on his artificial hand. He wore a half-length gray velvet cape lined with gray satin, and his feet were shod in gray velvet embroidered acrobat's shoes.

Marcel enhanced his mysterious, Mephisthophelean image by wearing a skintight black jumpsuit, whose sleeves were also slashed to reveal brilliant red fabric beneath. His waist was circled by a belt of rubies set in black leather, and his jet black hair was topped by a red velvet skullcap. His tall, spare frame was cloaked in a full-length black cape with red satin lining. These two dashing, handsome widowers were bound to attract the attention and interest of every eligible lady at the reception.

The limousine drove for about an hour, with neither of its passengers saying much from the back seat. Eventually a large dark hill loomed before them. "Is the Duke's castle on that mountain?" Etienne asked the chauffeur.

"The castle *is* the mountain" was the terse reply.

Rimskor Castle was indeed an imposing edifice. It rose an incredible 275 meters into the air, and the diameter at its base was over a hundred meters. Built out of structural steel and covered with aluminum and plastic, the outside of the castle was an artificial forest. Ersatz trees of gleaming metal dotted its slopes, while robot animals frolicked and gamboled among them. As an architectural achievement there was nothing to compare with it in this entire Sector of space.

There was only one way into the mountain, which was otherwise solid. The private roadway led up to an enormous arched gateway. An electrified gate, with vertical bars only twenty-five centimeters apart, stood in their path while their car was bathed in light from a series of spotlights directly over the entrance. Two armed guards stood inside the gate eyeing the party coldly until the chauffeur produced a small electronically coded plastic card and fitted it into a slot in the wall. As the gates swung slowly open, the chauffeur retrieved the card, tucked it into his pocket and drove the limousine past the guards and into the large garage that was the lowest level of the castle's interior.

There were already an enormous number of cars parked here, indicating that the reception must be going at full strength upstairs. The chauffeur held the car door open for the two men as they got out, and Marcel d'Alembert brushed slightly against the driver. "I want to thank you for your fine service, my good man," he said with dignity. "I trust it will be you who drives us back to the Circus when we leave."

"Me or one of the other chauffeurs on His Grace's staff, My Lord."

"No, I insist that it must be you. You did such an outstanding job that I would entrust the task to no other."

"As you wish, My Lord." And he showed them the way to the elevator tube.

"Did you get it?" Etienne whispered the instant they were alone.

In answer, Marcel d'Alembert slipped him the plastic entry card he had picked out of the chauffeur's pocket when he bumped him. Etienne took the piece of plastic and ran the fourth finger of his right hand lightly over its surface. The electronic sensing device inside that artificial digit read the coded pattern and recorded it for future reference. Then he handed the card back to his brother. "It'll be back in his pocket when we leave," Marcel said. "They won't suspect anything, so they won't change the gate code."

"What if he misses it in the meantime?"

"He'll find it eventually in that same pocket and think he just searched haphazardly before. Haven't you ever found something in a place where you thought you'd already looked for it? Just one of life's little frustrations. What about the defenses?"

Duke Etienne stroked his right pinkie finger lightly. "There's a heavy minefield on either side of the road. I detected pressure plates all along the roadway itself to let the guards know someone's coming. The road's mined, too, so that if the guards see someone approaching whom they don't like, they can blow him to smithereens."

Just then the doors to the elevator tube opened, cutting off further conversation, and the two brothers emerged into the main hallway. As was the case with the rest of the castle, this chamber had walls of metal that were polished to a perfect shine. Large jewels set in the walls reflected rainbow patterns all over the immense room. The arched ceiling was easily twenty meters over their heads and was composed of thousands of mirrors, so that their movements on the floor were reflected above them. There were several dozen people milling about in the hall, but both men knew that if the room had been empty their footsteps, even in their relatively soft shoes, would have resounded like gunshots in an echo chamber off the shiny metal floors.

A robot decked in fancy livery came over to them. The machine was standard for its type, being a meter and a half tall and roughly cylindrical, with numerous tentacular arms extending outward around its body. They showed it the invitations the Duke had sent them and it promptly announced them over the loudspeaker. In just a few moments, they could see the tall, thin machine-body of Duke Fyodor striding down the corridor to greet them personally. "How are you both? I'm so glad you could make it. My Lord Marcel, it's a pleasure to meet so talented a man. Your act yesterday was nothing short of superb."

"You put on a pretty good act yourself, Your Grace. This castle of yours has got to be one of the most incredible pieces of workmanship I've ever seen. It makes my own magic look puny by comparison."

The compliment was precisely the perfect thing to say, for Duke Fyodor beamed like a little boy winning a prize for having the best puppy in the show. This castle was obviously a labor of love for him, and to have it praised so enthusiastically opened his gates of cordiality. "I've done my best to make it unusual," he said. "Would you like me to show you around?"

"I'd like nothing better," Marcel said truthfully. "Right now, your castle is the most interesting thing in the Universe to me." He turned to his brother. "What about you?"

Etienne smiled. "Yes, I have to admit my own castle back on DesPlaines can't begin to compare with this. We have to build short and solid there, you know, because of the gravity. I'd be honored if you'd give us the grand tour."

"Right this way, then." Duke Fyodor began walking toward one end of the immense hallway, and the d'Alemberts followed after him, having to quicken their pace to

71

match their guide's giant strides. They passed by many elegantly dressed dignitaries who gave them curious glances, as though wondering who these two people were to be so singled out for the Duke's attentions.

"You will notice," the Duke continued as he led the way out of the public portion of the hall and into a more secluded area, "that I chose to build almost exclusively in metal and plastic. The great majority of my servants are robots, and a great deal of the maintenance around the castle is done by automation. Some of my critics have actually analyzed me using that as a basis, did you know that? Some nonsense about my having more of an affinity for machines than for people because it's machines that keep me alive; that because Nature has seemed to turn its back on me, that I in turn despise Nature and try to shut it out of my life. Bah, nothing could be further from the truth." There was a bright light glowing at the end of the hall, and as Fyodor led the two men into the room, both had to squint not to be blinded by the incredible sight.

"Behold," the Duke of Kolokov said. "Behold the Chamber of Angles, epitome of my creations."

The sheer spectacle left the two DesPlainians speechless. The room itself was gigantic; it must have occupied easily half the mountain that was Rimskor Castle. The ceiling was so high that Etienne would have had to strain his neck to try to see it. The base of the room was fully thirty meters across. Sloping ramps led from each of the various entranceways that were scattered about the perimeter all the way up to near the ceiling, ascending in a series of sharp, zigzag passages. The crazy angles jangled on the optic nerves of any rational human being who looked at them. The ramps were suspended from the ceiling by long stretches of girders, and the entire construction looked structurally unsound, as though a sharp gust of wind might topple everything.

Suspended from the ceiling also were large metal mobiles, seemingly thousands of them, all composed solely of acute angles and each one polished to reflect a jagged image around the room; the entire vast chamber was filled with pulsating, rotating sparks of whiteness that were the reflections of an intense beacon that beamed down from center ceiling. The room was almost hypnotic in its effect, and Etienne found that, after looking at it for only a few

72

seconds he had to turn his gaze resolutely to the polished metal floor. Marcel, possibly because of all his own work with illusions, was able to examine the room more closely, but even he had to bite his lips to keep from letting the vision eat away at his consciousness.

"Remarkable, isn't it?" Duke Fyodor asked proudly.

"It's . . . stunning," Etienne said, trying hard to come up with the most diplomatic word possible. "There never could have been anything like it before."

Their host took that as a compliment. "What I abhor is not Nature, but inefficiency. To me, beauty is precision. The precision of a machine going perfectly through its paces—or, in the case of your Circus, the precision of human beings performing their elaborate and dangerous acts with a smoothness that beggars the imagination. The Chamber of Angles is dedicated to the spirit of precision, to the mechanical . . . in short, to perfection."

"I think so much perfection must be an acquired taste," Etienne said. "Would you mind if we continued on with the rest of the tour? I feel so . . . so overwhelmed here."

"I understand," replied the Duke of Kolokov. "It *is* an awe-inspiring sight. Let me show you through some of the more prosaic parts of my domicile."

The "prosaic" portions of the castle, while less overwhelming than that chamber of insanity, were all nonetheless masterpieces of applied technology. The enormous kitchen, where meals for up to two hundred guests could be prepared, was a virtual assembly line of food preparation, with computer programs set to fix anything from a single deviled egg to six grosses of royal almondine layertorts. Dozens of little robots scampered here and there, none of them more than a meter high and all of them with at least six constantly busy hands.

"Note the dumbwaiter system," Duke Fyodor said with pride as he pointed to a large opening in one wall. "Food—or for that matter, any sort of package or container—can travel from here to any room in the castle. It's all inside the walls and out of sight. Invisible, efficient, and totally automated. Like the Chamber of Angles, it's my own design—and, if I do say so myself, it's virtually foolproof." The two guests inspected the system and marveled at it, then went on with the rest of the tour.

The bedrooms were harsh and utilitarian, filled with

mirrored walls and glaring lights. The constant use of metals made them all seem cold and impersonal, and Etienne doubted he would ever be able to fall asleep in such a room—he would be afraid he'd dream of robot bogeymen crawling out from under the bed and spiriting him away.

The library was imposing but, again, cold. Long shelves stretched from floor to ceiling, housing hundreds of thousands of bookreels with a detached, almost over-bearing elegance. The Duke of DesPlaines could not help but be reminded of his own collection of literary works, which traveled with him wherever he went. He collected books, the ancient examples of the art of printing and binding that was almost extinct in this twenty-fifth century. Admittedly, the books were heavier and took up more room than an equal number of bookreels; but there was something solid and substantial about them. The knowledge they contained seemed so much more real.

No matter how many twists and turns their course took them along, nor how many levels up and down they moved, Marcel d'Alembert's sharp mind kept exact track of where they were. With his inborn sense of direction, he was composing a mental map of the entire layout of the castle's interior. When they returned to the Circus later, he would transfer his map onto paper for the benefit of the assault team that would soon be invading this very stronghold.

"That's about all there is to see," Duke Fyodor said as he brought their tour to a conclusion by leading them back into a large hall filled with other guests. "My Lord Marcel, would you be so kind as to reciprocate by performing a portion of your marvelous act for my guests?"

"I'd be delighted," the magician said. "Just give me a couple of minutes to prepare." Duke Fyodor nodded and went off to find a servant who could make an announcement about the forthcoming entertainment.

To his brother, Marcel added quietly, "There's one area he didn't take us into; it's a big blank on my map. It's on this level, just off the eastern side of that enormous insanity of a room. The blank area's only one or two rooms deep, but it extends upward for at least eight stories."

"Do you think there's something in there our host doesn't want us to see?"

74

"It bears investigating. He's been eager enough to show us everything else in the place; why not that?" He stopped talking as he heard his name being called out. "That sounds like my cue to go on. Wish me luck."

"You wish *me* luck. I'll need it more than you will." Etienne smiled at his brother as Marcel made his way through the crowd to the front of the room where an impromptu stage had been arranged for him.

"Thank you for your attention, ladies and lords," the performer began. "I have been called, at times, the greatest magician in the Galaxy. I know it isn't true, but what does my opinion matter against that of so many others? But, if I am a great magician I owe it all to my audiences—to you. You see, no magician could perform without the unconscious aid of the people he's performing for. For instance—you, gospodin," and he stepped up to a man standing in the first row, "I've never met you before, have I? And you think that, because I've singled you out, I'm going to somehow use you to perform a magical feat. Actually—" and here he pulled a large bouquet of flowers seemingly from the ear of the woman standing next to the man "—I'm going to use her. Excuse me, madame, but these are for you." He bowed low and presented the bouquet to the startled matron, to a round of laughter and applause.

"Misdirection is the key," he continued when the reaction had subsided. "I can do anything I choose and you won't ever see it because your attention is focused exactly where I want it to be. That's how you all help me, by following my suggestions so well. Say, for example, that I asked you to watch my right hand." He held up that hand with an exaggerated gesture, and every eye in the room fixed on it. "I want you to look there, because the trick is really being done with my left." To prove it, he held up his left hand, which now held a lighted candle. Again there was laughter and applause.

This was Etienne's cue. As Marcel had said so well, misdirection was the key. While every guest at the party was watching the performance with rapt attention, the Duke of DesPlaines was able to vanish down the hall without anyone's noticing his disappearance.

Moving as quietly as he could down the long corridor, he came once again to the Chamber of Angles. As his brother had pointed out, there was one door on the east side that appeared to be locked. Etienne walked over to it, but did not touch it or attempt to open it in any way. Instead, he ran the pinkie finger of his artificial right hand around the doorsill, about a centimeter from the surface. Just as he suspected, the sensitive instruments inside that synthetic digit detected an electronic lock and alarm system of a fairly high degree of complexity. He did not have with him the tools he would need to break in there, but that was a minor point—such tools were on hand back at the Circus.

Marcel had said that this locked area extended upward for several stories. Leaning backwards and craning his neck, he tried to see if there was a door leading from this chamber to one of the upper levels. There did seem to be one three floors up, but the very act of looking brought back the panicky sensation Etienne had first felt upon entering this room. The hackles raised on his skin and he had to shut his eyes to avoid the glare and the dizzying effects. Alone, with his eyes closed and the room completely silent, he could sense, rather than hear, the strange vibrations. *Subsonics, more than likely,* he thought. Vibrations in the air at a frequency inaudible to the human ear but strong enough to affect a person's nervous system. No wonder the room felt eerie—it was all part of Duke Fyodor's plan to impress people. He probably enjoyed putting visitors into an uncomfortable position.

Knowing the room's secret made it a little less frightening, but the subsonics still made him edgy despite himself. He made his way over to one of the ramps that led up to the level of the door he wanted. He checked the metal ramp with his pinkie finger before ascending, but there were no alarms on it, nor was it electrified. The ramps were no more than they appeared to be—a means of going by foot from one level to another.

The ramp swayed ever so slightly as he trod upon it, but otherwise seemed stable enough. He could feel the vibrations of the room coming even stronger through the soles of his feet as he began to climb up the steep slope. The ramp went through four abrupt changes of direction along the path before he reached the level he wanted; four sharp turns through impossibly acute angles. And with each level upward, the vibrations increased measurably in strength, so that by the time he reached the desired height, Etienne felt his body trembling involuntarily. Duke Fyodor had planned the defenses of this room subtly but well.

Much to his surprise, this doorway was neither locked nor switched into an alarm circuit; apparently, Duke Fyodor put enough faith in the subsonics to discourage visitors to the upper floors—or was it that he was sure most intruders would go for the lower door first? Whichever way it was, Etienne was not going to pass up an opportunity to see what lay behind the door in that area where the host would not take them.

He opened the door and saw only darkness on the other side. He didn't dare switch on the light whose button was beside the door, since that action might alert anyone inside. Again, he should leave that job to those who would be following after him; they would be better equipped for this sort of work.

He had just closed the door and started down the ramp again when a loud voice boomed out, "Hey! What are you doing up there?"

The head of the d'Alembert clan raised his right hand and pointed the forefinger in the direction of the sound. That particular digit was a deadly one, concealing a miniature blaster. At any hint of trouble, Etienne was prepared to blast his way out and explain the messy details later.

The speaker had been a robot, one of the tiny machines that had been serving refreshments out in the main ballroom. Since it had a limited function, it probably had a limited intelligence to go with it, and had probably been on its way to the kitchen when it had spotted him. With any luck, he should be able to bluff his way out.

Lowering his hand, Duke Etienne wavered back and forth and feigned a spell of dizzyness. "I was looking . . . for a fresher. Saw this door up here, climbed up . . . feel very weak, dizzy." As he spoke, he began staggering down the ramp, hoping to confuse the dim-witted machine into inaction. Each step away from the door would be a step in his favor; it was proximity to that forbidden portal that was most suspicious, and convincing the robot that he had no sinister intentions would probably mean that the machine would not report him.

"You have no right to be up there," the machine said.

"Sorry, I felt so . . . so dizzy I didn't know what I was doing." Etienne was halfway down the ramp now, and feeling safer with each step.

"Only authorized personnel are allowed up there," the robot reiterated. It was a machine of limited intelligence but fierce tenacity.

"You're right, of course," Etienne said, reaching the bottom of the ramp. "Whew. I feel much better down here now," he added truthfully. "I owe your master the Duke a profound apology for trespassing in his castle without permission. Would you be so kind as to tell me where he is so that I may go offer my apologies at once?"

This maneuver confused the poor device. If this strange person were a burglar—an as yet unproven hypothesis anyway—then he was not acting in approved burglar fashion. Asking to be told where the master of the castle was didn't seem to be regulation behavior for criminals. After about thirty seconds of whirling that data around in its computerized circuits, the robot decided that the intruder must be what he said he was—a stranger who got lost looking for a fresher. "His Grace the Duke is in the ballroom, watching a magic act," it said, then continued trundling on its way to the kitchen. The matter of the inruder was now banished from its feeble mind.

Etienne breathed a sigh of relief and made his way back to the main entertainment area. His primary mission had been accomplished. Rimskor Castle had been reconnoitered and the approximate location of possible clues had been determined. More fact finding would have to await a more serious assault by a team of d'Alemberts in better condition than the two patriarchs of the clan.

In the meantime, he could enjoy watching the conclusion of his brother's act.

Chapter 7

Stalking

The second day of the Progress looked as beautiful as the first, but the two d'Alemberts were in no real condition to appreciate it. Both had been up most of the night, comparing notes and checking out the premises from top to bottom. Yvette had been along every centimeter of the corridor in the wing of the castle where Edna was staying, her electronic gadgetry out and working. Every crevice, every small hole in the plaster, every picture frame, every piece of furniture was examined in minute detail. She gained some red lines infiltrating the whites of her eyes and an intimate acquaintance with the architecture of Rockhold Castle, but there was no other reward for her efforts.

Jules's search was also fruitless. While Borov was in the hospital for observation on his ribs, Jules took the liberty of going through that candidate's room with his own detectors. He checked all the personal belongings, all the clothing, the luggage, and the furniture in the room where Borov might have stashed a bomb. Nothing. If Borov actually was the assassin, he had taken the bomb with him to the hospital. It would be a dangerous move—but then, the traitor was playing for dangerous stakes.

Of course, it was entirely possible that Borov was not the traitor—in which case, Jules had only a dozen other suspects to worry about.

He and Yvette discussed the problem. "Edna's wing is clean," Yvette said, "and the security is so tight I don't see how anyone could sneak in there to plant a bomb, even a tiny one." She sighed with frustration. "I don't think we're doing so well on this assignment, *mon cher frère*. There's got to be something we've overlooked, or else the threat is coming from some entirely new direction that we know nothing about."

Jules felt equally frustrated, and pounded his right fist into his left palm. "Maybe. Maybe. I've learned to trust your intuition. But that still doesn't give us any clue about what we *are* looking for, and until we can come up with something better we'll have to continue along with our only lead."

"And in the meantime we stay around the Princess all day and skulk around the castle all night. If we don't find the traitor in the first three days, I think I'm going to drop from exhaustion."

The two siblings parted then, to return to their respective rooms and try to get at least a couple of hours' sleep before they had to go back on duty the next morning.

At breakfast, Crown Princess Edna was presented with a beautiful paper flower by Choyen Liu. "It's lovely," she exclaimed. "Where did you get it?"

"I made it last night," he replied. "The petals represent the unfolding of the soul around the center of essential being."

"Oh." That was all the Princess could think to say for a long second. "Thank you very much. I appreciate it. It's very much like you."

"You're too kind. It's but a useful object for meditation."

As she sat down to breakfast with Yvette beside her, Edna placed the artificial bloom in such a way that the female d'Alembert could check it out more closely. With seemingly casual gestures, Yvette moved her camouflaged miniaturized sensors to within a couple of centimeters of the object, but it was exactly what it seemed to be. Yvette gave a slight nod of approval, and Edna pinned the paper flower to the shoulder of her tunic.

The previous day's activities at the beach had taken a higher toll on people than they had realized. No precautions had been taken against the solar rays and, as a result, nearly everyone in the party from the Princess on

80

down was complaining of mild sunburn. The only two who escaped that fate were Symond and Liu.

"Anares' sun is green, and hotter than this one," Liu remarked when questioned. "I'm used to far more radiation than I'm receiving."

"My own skin is kind of funny," explained the blond, fair-complexioned Symond in turn. "Either nothing at all happens or else I burn up completely. I guess I was just lucky yesterday." All the others in the party agreed with that assessment.

The activity for the day was supposed to be a hunt in the small forest half a kilometer from Rockhold. When the schedule had originally been made, both Jules and Yvette had protested vigorously the inclusion of such an activity. "It's bad enough," Yvette declared, "that we might have to be dealing with someone who wants to blow you up. But going out in a group of armed people is ridiculous. Jules and Jacques and Yvonne and I—and even your other bodyguards as well—can't keep an eye on everyone at once. One quick shot would be all that's needed."

"Zander said that everything should be done as normally as possible," Edna maintained. "It's been well reported in the press that I enjoy hunting. Our suspect might become suspicious if there wasn't any during the Progress. And besides, *everyone* will be armed. The killer might hesitate knowing that everyone around him has a weapon, too. If he missed, he wouldn't get another chance."

In the end, of course, the Princess won out, though she did agree to the d'Alemberts' suggestion that the hunt be scheduled fairly early during the Progress. Their thinking was that the assassin would still be acting conservatively then; he might pass up a chance at shooting her if he thought he might get a better opportunity later. If the hunt were scheduled toward the end of the Progress, he might decide he wouldn't *get* a better chance.

Borov joined them shortly after breakfast, just as they were about to leave on their expedition. The pain of his broken ribs and the disappointment at missing some of his time on the Progress had done nothing to improve his disposition. He was sullen and complained loudly about the terrible service he had received at the hospital. Yvette and Edna exchanged disgusted glances, but said nothing.

The party set out into the forest. Because of the trouble

they had had the previous day with the dorvats, they rode in cars today instead. They parked their vehicles at the edge of the woods and walked the rest of the way, which meant that the candidate who'd sprained his ankle the previous day was unable to accompany them. To the people who had to protect the Princess that was a bit of relief, because it meant one less suspect they'd have to keep an eye on.

The party marched along through the cool forest, delighting in the freshness of the air and the pleasantness of the breeze. The natural scents of plants and animals commingled in the atmosphere, producing a euphoric bouyancy in the spirits of the group, which had still been a bit low from the mishap of the day before.

The forest was full of game of all sizes, up to and including panna-cats, the fastest and most feared predators of the planet. To make the event more sporting, all the participants were issued old-fashioned projectile weapons rather than stunners, which were too easy to hit the target with. Projectile weapons required much more skill and accuracy to handle properly.

A point system had been set up based on the size of the animal, its speed, and how many shots were needed to kill it. By courtesy, the spotter was always granted the right of the first shot; after that, the kill was open to anyone who could make it.

After only two hours they had bagged a fair amount of game. Almost all of it was little rabbitlike creatures called bobbers. What they lacked in size they made up for in speed, and they were deceptively hard targets to hit. Edna herself had gotten three of them, as opposed to two each for Jules, Borov, and Symond, and one by nearly every one of the other candidates. In addition, the Princess had felled a whiteneck—a small herbivore that, at full growth, was the size of an Earthly fawn. Whiteneck meat was considered a delicacy by Ansegria's gourmets, and Edna was justly congratulated on her prowess at the hunt.

Most of the morning was spent quietly, with no one bothering to say much—ostensibly to avoid frightening the game. Only the sounds of occasional gunshots disturbed the general silence—and at each sound, the two d'Alemberts and the two Roumeniers cringed and looked first to the Princess. But none of the shots were aimed at her.

Edna, oblivious to their concern, had immersed herself

82

totally in the excitement of the hunt. Her face was aglow with energy, her muscles were taut with expectation. Most of the time she walked beside Paul Symond, and even though the two of them did not speak much there was a communication between them on an extremely basic level. Symond obviously enjoyed this pastime as much as she did; the same hunter's gleam could be detected in his eyes, the same enthusiastic spring livened his steps. When he smiled, it was a smile of warmth, and an unspoken conversation flowed between their eyes when they looked at one another.

When they stopped for lunch in a small clearing, Edna commented to Choyen Liu that he alone of the candidates had not managed to shoot anything. "That," he replied solemnly, "is because I do not believe in killing creatures for sport."

"But you're not a vegetarian, I've seen you eat meat."

"It's a question of destiny. Food animals are raised by human beings for the express purpose of being killed for their substance. For me to deny that would be closing my eyes to their destiny—in essence, refusing to take my place in the chain of life.

"But these animals here in the forest have their own destinies, independent of us. To hunt them down at random on our own whims is to interfere with their destinies—to interfere in a business which should not concern us."

Edna was starting to pick up the hang of Liu's little philosophical games. He was verbally sparring with her, and in a strange way she found it exhilarating. It was as though he were asking something more of her than she'd ever thought of giving before. Rising to his challenge, she countered, "But couldn't it be the creature's destiny to be killed by your gun?"

Liu smiled, pleased that Edna had entered the game. "Not if I don't pull the trigger," he said and, bowing, walked off to eat lunch by himself—leaving in his wake a very puzzled crown princess wondering exactly what was going on inside his mind.

"Don't worry about him," Borov said. "He's been making those mystic pronouncements of his ever since he arrived here. Nobody listens anymore."

"I listen," Edna said coldly. "There's probably more

meaning in the sighing of the wind than in the screeching of a peacock." She didn't realize until after she'd said it how close her phraseology was to the Anarian's style of proverb. Blinking with amazement at her own profundity, she walked away and left Borov standing angrily in the center of the clearing.

"I think I'm becoming as mystical as Choyen Liu," the Princess said to Yvette as she sat down with her to eat her lunch. "I'm starting to talk like he does . . . and he's starting to make a little sense!"

When lunch was over, the group started out again, hoping to run into slightly bigger game than they'd encountered in the morning. Borov hung to the back, staying well clear of Liu. The pain in his ribs and the Princess's icy remark had worn a thin edge on his temper, and the resulting vehemence came out directed at Liu. Every so often he would make a caustic remark about how the Anarian was trying to cover up his lack of skill by saying he was ethically opposed to hunting. His comments became increasingly louder, until there was no way the Anarian could have avoided hearing them; but still Liu paid no notice of the insults and walked along the ground with his rifle dangling casually over his arm.

This lack of response annoyed Borov worse than if Liu had returned the insults in kind. He felt he was being ignored, one of the worst possible fates imaginable to a show-off like himself. Finally he lost his temper altogether. "Liu!" he called out loudly. "Turn around and look at me, you cowardly pligworm. Let me see if you can face anything like a man."

Edna, who had been doing her diplomatic best to also ignore Borov's taunts all afternoon, whirled angrily, about to chastise the man. But she found Liu already facing Borov, a look of serenity engraved on his imperturbable features. "What seems to be your problem?" the Anarian asked in even tones.

Borov was somewhat unnerved by this casual acceptance of his challenge, but he was too far into this confrontation to back out now without loss of face. Stubbornly he continued. "I don't think you deserve to be along on this Progress. Edna needs a man to mate with, not a burrowing nightcrawler like you."

Without warning, Liu raised his rifle in Borov's direction

and fired. The bullet whizzed just past the Kolokovnik's head, startling the daylights out of him and stoking the fires of his anger still further. "You murderous cretin!" he bellowed. "I'll kill you."

In the heat of his anger he dropped his gun and charged straight at the Anarian like an enraged bull at a matador's cape. He never got there, though; both Jules and Symond were in positions between the two men, and both sprang instantly into action to prevent a worse fight. Symond was closer to Borov than Jules was, and consequently bore the brunt of the attack. Borov's fists pummeled his body with blind fury, and Symond was hard-pressed to defend himself. Instead, he retreated strategically, giving ground before the other's onslaught and allowing Jules to get into position. It took only one hard punch from the Des-Plainian's powerful fist to knock Borov to the ground where he lay for a minute, still conscious but quite stunned.

Edna stalked over to him and stood beside his body as it was sprawled out on the ground. "Gospodin Borov," she said in a chilled voice as soon as she was sure the words would register, "this is the most disgraceful exhibition I've ever watched. I know I told you not to treat me like a princess; but this irascible, egotistical, unmanly conduct would not be fitting in front of even my lowliest serving maid. You are dishonored, *tovarishch*, and as such you can be no fit company for us. You are to return to Rockhold, pack your belongings, and leave at once. I never want to see you again."

"But what about him?" Borov exploded, pointing at Liu. "He took a shot at me. Doesn't he get punished?"

"Look behind you, Borov," Jules said quietly.

Borov turned his head scornfully, looked on the grass about three meters behind where he'd been standing, and suddenly gasped. Lying there stretched out its full two-and-a-half-meter length was the body of a panna-cat. The slight breeze ruffled its short coat of yellow-green fur, and its powerful paws twitched spasmodically, as it was still in its death throes. There was only a small spot of blood staining that magnificent creature—right between the eyes, where Liu's single shot had hit true to its mark and buried itself in the animal's brain.

"In another second," Jules said, "it would have leaped at you. I saw it about the same time Liu did, but he was

85

already facing in the right direction, so he got off the only shot possible in time—a perfect one, I might add. So much for your thinking he's a weakling or a coward." He reached down a hand and yanked Borov roughly to his feet. "Now, you heard Edna—get out of our sight."

There was still lightning behind Borov's eyes. "I'll get you for this, Dallum," he warned. "And you, Symond. And particularly you, Liu. We've got a score to settle, you and I."

"So help me," Edna said with barely restrained fury, "if I or anyone on this Progress catches you around this area trying to make trouble, you'll be sent to Gastonia for treason without benefit of trial. Without benefit of a spaceship, either, if I have my way. Now go!"

There could be no questioning the imperial tone of her voice. If there had been any doubt at all in the minds of anyone present, it was now banished for good. This relatively plain-looking young woman was born to rule the Empire of Earth. Every inflection, every gesture commanded instant obedience.

Borov slunk off the scene like the whipped dog he was, figurative tail between his legs. But Jules could not help noticing the glare of resentment still held deep within those eyes.

Without Borov along, the afternoon passed quite easily and uneventfully. Both Jules and Yvette, while admitting that Edna had had no other choice but to banish Borov, were unhappy it had come to that. He was still a suspect as the bomber, and now they would no longer be able to keep an eye on his activities. Then too, if he hadn't been planning on killing Edna before, the new set of circumstances might make that idea seem acceptable to him. As Jules put it when he found a moment to talk to the Princess privately, "When your life's already in danger, it doesn't make much sense to antagonize people or make new enemies."

"I appreciate your concern," Edna answered, "but what else was I to do? Order had to be maintained or the entire Progress would have fallen apart. And a person in command can't help but make enemies—I've learned that lesson well enough at Court by this time. Borov's no threat to me, though I am a little worried that he might take after you or Symond or Liu."

"Don't worry," said Jacques Roumenier, butting into the conversation. "I'll alert the guards and see to it that he doesn't bother any of us again."

By the time they were finished with the hunt, Symond had won the honors as best hunter by obtaining the most points. Edna was second, only two points behind him. Jules was fifth—but then, he had not been trying very hard.

Back at Rockhold, dinner was served in people's rooms. This was done so that they would have more time to prepare for the evening's entertainment, which was to be a formal ball. Though, to be perfectly honest, none of the Progress's participants was in a festive mood. The events of the last two days weighed heavily on everyone.

Nevertheless, they were all dressed in their most scintillating array when they arrived in the ballroom at the appointed hour. Princess Edna, of course, looked the most resplendent of the group. The bodice of her gown was of a rich oyster white brocade and was trimmed with gold and emeralds; the dress consisted of wide strips of that same brocade gathered together at the waist and flowing free to the floor. As she moved, the strips would rustle and part to reveal a petticoat of emerald green satin. The gown's large puffed sleeves were slit, and undersleeves of the same green satin showed through. Edna wore her hair in braids piled high atop her head 'and, instead of a tiara, she wore an heirloom necklace of gold filigree and emeralds displayed across her forehead as a pendant. Tiny pearl earrings were the only other jewelry she wore—but then, she was the Crown Princess and didn't have to show off.

Edna was not the only well-dressed person in the hall, however. Her ladies-in-waiting all had their own High Court gowns, and even the bodyguards looked impressive in their formal black and red uniforms. And the clothes of the different candidates had been bought by the dukes of their respective planets; no expense had been spared to make them look as dashing and handsome as could be. Each candidate was dressed according to the latest fashion on his home world, representing a breathtaking array of styles and fabrics. Velvet robes, brocade vests, satin tunics with tights, fur-lined capes, glittering jewelry—all were in evidence within the large ballroom. The complete spectrum of colors was presented in a kaleidoscopic pattern as the ball's participants swirled gracefully around the floor.

Even Choyen Liu, normally the most conservative dresser of the lot, looked impressive. The tight gold lamé pants clung to every curve of his leg, and his dark brown shirt was hand embroidered with gold thread and intricate, almost hypnotic, patterns and spirals.

As host and hostess, Baron Piers and Baroness Ximena led off the first dance, moving with an astonishing grace that belied their years. The rest of the party applauded as they finished their turn, then moved onto the dance floor in pairs to commence their own dancing. Edna chose Paul Symond as her first partner. Theoretically, that choice was meaningless, since she would have to dance at least once during the evening with each of the candidates. But the fact that she had chosen this one man did not go unnoticed by the rest. Already, the trend could be seen that she was tending to prefer Symond's smooth, easy style to all the others, and none of them was particularly happy about it.

Outside, a pair of sinister eyes watched from a tree limb through a window as events transpired in the ballroom. Anton Borov had been feeling entirely too angry at being evicted from the Progress to let his disgrace go unavenged. He had been spoiled rotten all his life; he had always won at whatever he attempted. And to fail so miserably in this endeavor was too strong a blow to his pride to be ignored.

The guards around the grounds were extra alert because of his threats that afternoon, but even so he had little difficulty slipping past them and into the garden that overlooked the wing of the castle where the ballroom was located. Rockhold Castle had never been intended as a fortress, and had not been built with an eye for security. Even with his ribs searing fire through the right side of his body, Borov was still in good enough shape to get past the guards and hide in a tree in the garden, biding his time until he could make his move.

He watched dance after dance take place inside that ballroom, and he kept wishing he were there. He was such a superb dancer that the Princess could not have helped being taken with his charms and skills if she'd only had one dance with him. Finally there was a break in the dancing, and people came out into the garden for some fresh air, singly or in pairs. Borov saw one of his quarry go off by himself to one of the more secluded portions of the garden. He smiled. That corner of the grounds was hidden from the main house by a stand of small trees and bushes. No one would be able to see him there.

He slipped silently down out of the tree and glided along the path after his victim, a sinister shadow in the night. He reached into his pocket and pulled out his weapon, enjoying the smooth, hard feel of the stun-gun in his hand. It brought vitality back into his being. It would be his means of avenging himself of these other men who had disgraced him and his planet so severely.

He and the man he was pursuing were out of sight now, the perfect time for an ambush. With such an opportunity for a clear shot, Borov dared not waste it. The distance between them was less than five meters. Raising his stunner, Borov fired its ray directly into the back of his quarry.

The other man stopped, and Borov's jaw dropped in surprise. His stun-gun had been set on eight; the victim should have instantly fallen to the ground and been paralyzed for days—possibly permanently crippled. Instead, the stunner beam had seemed to have no effect whatsoever on the man, except that its low buzzing sound had told him that someone was shooting at him.

Borov was too stunned to move. He could only continue firing his stunner uselessly as the other figure turned and, with a demonic smile on his face, began advancing relentlessly on his erstwhile attacker.

The dancing had started up again inside the ballroom. It was Jules's turn to dance with Edna, and the two of them were quietly enjoying each other's company. They exchanged the smiles of two people who shared a secret that others around them didn't know. For Edna, this was also a chance to relax; Jules was not really a candidate for her hand, so she didn't have to put on a show for his benefit, nor did she have to be constantly sizing him up as prospective matrimonial material. She could be herself with him, and that feeling was immensely satisfying.

Suddenly a loud cry of alarm sounded from outside. "Somebody, come quickly!" called a voice that the Des-Plainians recognized as belonging to Jacques.

Immediately the hall began emptying as everyone rushed to see what had happened. Edna's first impulse was to rush outside also, but Jules squeezed her hand gently. "It could be a diversion," he warned.

Yvette and Yvonne came running up to the two of them; their first duty was the Princess's safety. "Vonnie, *ma cherie,* you stay with Edna. Don't let her do anything stupid like running outside and getting her head blown off. Come on, Evie, let's take a look."

There was a crowd gathered around the bottom of a hill in the garden by the time they arrived. Pushing through the mob, they made their way to the front where Yvonne's brother Jacques was waiting for them. He didn't say a word, nor did he have to. The scene at his feet was startling enough.

There, stretched out on the ground, was the body of Anton Borov, quite dead. His mouth was open and an expression of horror was frozen on his features. And lying across his body, which was oozing blood, was the entire trunk of a large banabol tree.

Chapter 8

Invasion Force

Duke Etienne d'Alembert and his brother Marcel spent most of the day after their return from Rimskor Castle in conference together. They had, after all, a great deal to discuss. Both of them agreed that Duke Fyodor, while outwardly polite and sensible, was standing right on the borderline of insanity. His obsession with the mechanical, the precise, the straight but slightly askew, was an indication of incipient mental imbalance. They also agreed that he was potentially dangerous, and that he was quite capable of formulating a plot to destroy the Crown Princess—though what his motive could be, they had not the faintest idea.

They talked about Rimskor Castle and about its defenses. Neither could ever recall seeing a stronghold so ingeniously designed to keep out intruders—a place whose very construction seemed to make forcible secret entry an impossibility. Not only was there but one way into the castle, but the road leading up to it was booby-trapped and under constant surveillance. Inside were enough alarms to make a bank security officer jealous. Only the most foolhardy, the most desperate, or the most capable of operatives would even seriously consider an assault on such a fortress.

Etienne and Marcel were not foolhardy or, at this stage of the game, particularly desperate. But they were two of the most capable tactical planners the Service of the Empire had ever known; and they knew that whatever tactics they planned would be carried out by members of the Family d'Alembert, the most capable, most talented single group of human beings alive.

They first ruled themselves out of further participation in the raid, for several reasons. For one thing, they were getting a little too old for such adventures, and both of them were smart enough to realize that. While each was still capable of taking on several people his own size or better, this particular raid would require the swiftness and surehandedness of youth. Their own contribution—experience—could be performed beforehand on the sidelines.

For another thing, they were already known inside Rimskor Castle. If, by some chance, they should be caught, the entire cover identity of the Circus as SOTE's right arm would be blown. Never in all the history of the Service had the Circus's true role been compromised. References to it were never written down, nor had its members ever even been listed on SOTE's computer files, lest some clever criminal someday tap into the computer memory. Thus, only the Imperial Family, the Head, and his daughter/factotum Helena knew the full story of the Circus's involvement in galactic security. If that involvement were to continue at its efficient level, no one else could be allowed to know. So Rimskor Castle would have to be invaded by people who were totally unknown there.

Once the two brothers had their plans mapped out, they decided on the personnel who would carry out the raid. With nearly a thousand members of the family to choose from, the selection of the assault team could have taken hours; but fortunately there were some specific talents they were looking for, and they were able to pick the appropriate people quite quickly. After the final show of the evening, Etienne and Marcel assembled the four chosen members in the manager's office for their briefing. The people were:

Rick d'Alembert, the leader of the wrestling team, who had already proven himself as being both durable and agile on many past assignments. His large, supermuscled form would give the team all the strength it would need.

Claude d'Alembert, a third-nephew of the Duke's, and one of the first-string members of the aerialist team that was the premiere act of the show. Like most DesPlainians, Claude was short and solidly built, yet even so there appeared to be a wiry quality to him. The speed of his reflexes was second to none in the Galaxy, and he could perform feats that ordinary mortals would consider impossible.

Jeanne d'Alembert, a second-niece to both Etienne and Marcel. At only age seventeen she was considered the Galaxy's most able animal tamer. Her complexion was quite pale and—for a DesPlainian—she was actually quite fragile, standing but one and a half meters tall and massing fifty-five kilograms. But despite the fact that physically she was the slightest of the Circus's personnel, her talents for handling animals would more than make up for her deficiencies.

And, finally, there was Luise deForrest, who had done such a capable job of leading the investigation that had led to the discovery of Duke Fyodor's involvement in the plot against the Princess. Duke Etienne was counting on her leadership abilities and quick, incisive mind to take charge and coordinate this mission—and hopefully find the evidence the family would need to smash Duke Fyodor's plans wide open.

The four members of the assault team stood rigidly alert in the Circus manager's office. All were dressed, at the Duke's insistence, in silver lamé jumpsuits; that color, he felt, would make them more inconspicuous while invading a place like Rimskor. On their feet they wore silver suregrip athletic shoes, which would give them a maximum amount of traction yet make a minimum amount of noise. All of them had belts with utility pouches for holding their specialized equipment—as well as blasters and stunners. In addition, Jeanne had, tucked within the bosom of her jumpsuit, one of her pets, who would make a fifth member of their team when the proper moment came.

"Part of our problem," Etienne was explaining, "is that we don't know exactly what we're looking for. We need some evidence of treason, obviously. If you can find a description of the time bomb—or where it's going to be set, or when, or by whom—that would be ideal, but don't hold out for that. Even the word 'bomb' on a scrap of paper would be enough to justify our intervention. The instant you find anything, send out a call on the bleeper. We'll rush in with blasters blazing. Give us the proof and we'll do the rest."

Then he and Marcel outlined the plan they had devised for the four invaders to break into Rimskor Castle. They sketched out what traps they were likely to encounter and how to circumvent them. Marcel provided them with a map of the castle, which they all memorized in a few minutes. *"Eh bien,"* Luise remarked when there was nothing more to be said, "let's get moving. Sitting here won't catch us a traitor."

They took one of the Circus's cars and drove through the night to the artificial mountain that was the castle. Actually, they drove right past it, and continued past for half a kilometer, where they parked their vehicle and doubled back on foot. That car could only have gotten in by going through the front gate—and they had not been invited.

The only way they could avoid being seen was to stay away from the road that led up to the entrance. Fortunately, Duke Fyodor had provided a ready way for them to do that. The entire outside of the "mountain" had been landscaped in metal and plastic as an artificial model of a real one. Rocks, outcroppings, and metallic trees abounded, making it easy for the d'Alemberts to form a mountain-climbing expedition.

Claude led them off. As the acrobat, he was the most agile of the quartet. Using the grappler hooks, ropes, and pulleys from his pouch as only a professional could, he made his way up the mountainside as easily as a mosquito up a pane of glass. This being the back side of the mountain, away from the entrance, there were no alarms. Why should there be, when the only way into the castle was still through an electrified, barred gate and two live guards?

Once Claude had gotten into a secure position, he helped pull the others up. Rick came next, then Jeanne, with Luise, the leader, holding up the rear in case of trouble. Having gotten this far, they proceeded to work their way around the mountainside to the front. They learned to avoid the metal trees, whose leaves were quite sharp and painful. Their path involved climbing around or over boulders and sometimes having to use the grapplers and ropes again to

94

climb higher on the slope in order to maneuver around one particular area.

On one such occasion, Claude was pulling himself upward along the rope when he ran afoul of one of the mechanical "mountain goats" that dwelled in this terrain. The goat, which had been programmed to be as cross as its natural counterpart, took exception to this intrusion on its exclusive territory, and proceeded to try to remedy the situation. Its major method of attack was to butt Claude with its head while the acrobat was hanging free on his rope. Claude could only hang on and swing out into empty air—and a possible thirty-meter fall—as the robot animal battered his body again and again.

Seeing what was happening, Rick drew his blaster to destroy the creature that was impeding their progress. "No," Luise whispered, putting her hand on his to stop him. "Blasting one of those things might just set off an alarm—or at least make someone curious enough to come out here and look. We've got to do it another way. Throw a rock at it."

Rick at first thought she was joking, but then realized she meant it. Looking around, he found a loose boulder that appeared adequate. It turned out to be lighter than it looked, being of an aluminum alloy, so it was no effort at all for his superbly trained body to lift the boulder and fling it at the goat. The missile was right on target, and hit the mechanical beast squarely in its midsection. The goat was startled at this unexpected assault, gave a tinny bleat, and wandered off along the mountainside, its pride more wounded than its body. With that obstacle surmounted, Claude began to climb once more.

"Everything all right?" Luise whispered up to him.

"Smooth. The ribs hurt a little, but I'll manage. Just keep the mosquitos away next time, eh?"

On they went, without further interruption, until they reached a projecting ledge just above the front gate. Below them they could see the searchlights that illuminated the narrow road leading up to the castle's entrance, and directly beneath the overhang would be the barred, electrified gate they would have to pass through to enter the castle—a gate covered with alarms, and whose bars were only twenty-five centimeters apart.

It was at this point that Jeanne's expertise came into

play. From out of the bosom of her silver lamé jumpsuit she pulled Bur-Bur, a small brown ticklemouse from the planet Corian. Bur-Bur was a little ball of fluff fifteen centimeters long and only twenty wide. When tucked inside Jeanne's clothing, all soft and warm and cuddly, he had just been a small ball of fur, lying quite still. When active, he would scamper around on his six tiny legs and look up at a person with those big black eyes that seemed three sizes too huge for his body. The ticklemice were considered vermin on their native world, but Corian had largely solved that problem now by exporting the cute creatures to other planets as pets.

It was not Bur-Bur's cuddliness, though, that had induced Jeanne to bring him along, but rather the fact that, despite his small size, the ticklemouse was an exceedingly intelligent creature—as smart or smarter than a terrestrial housecat, and infinitely more trainable.

As the other three members of the assault team waited, Jeanne "talked" to Bur-Bur. The conversation was mostly silent, with Jeanne cooing to the small animal, staring into his large eyes with her own and building the psychic bond between herself and him that was necessary for her own peculiar brand of magic to work. No one—least of all Jeanne—could ever explain how she had developed such a fantastic rapport with all kinds of animals; all her family knew was that it worked.

When she felt Bur-Bur was ready, she took out of her pouch a small mechanical device and strapped it on his back like a tiny saddle. Then, putting him down on the ground, she watched him scurry away to perform his assignment. The clever little beast picked his way carefully but quickly down the mountain slope alongside the gate. As they watched, the four d'Alemberts donned the gas masks they'd brought along and waited for developments to occur.

Bur-Bur reached the ground and, after standing up on his hindmost legs and sniffing the air, dashed rapidly forward inside the gate. Luise waited just a second to make sure he was inside, then pressed a button on a remote control device at her belt. The box on Bur-Bur's back flew open and emitted the characteristic sweet fumes of tirascaline, one of the strongest sleeping gases known to man. It would not affect the ticklemouse's nervous system at all, but the gas would knock out any human being in a matter of seconds and keep him unconscious for hours.

The invasion group didn't even wait for the effects to occur before starting down from their perch. It took them all of ten seconds to scramble to the ground, and by that time the two guards were completely oblivious to the world around them. Luise peered inside the gate just to make sure there were no other people—or robots—around, then began the next phase of the invasion.

Taking from her utility pouch the electronically coded plastic card that Marcel had duplicated, she inserted it into the slot beside the gate. Sure enough, the gate slid open to admit the party and the four of them raced inside. Jeanne picked up Bur-Bur, who was standing around after his mission was completed, wondering what to do next. She tucked him into the bosom of her jumpsuit and zipped it up to the top. Reassured that he had performed well, the tickle-mouse curled up and went back to sleep in his warm, pleasant surroundings.

The first stage of their plan had worked. They were actually inside Rimskor Castle.

Stage Two, however, would be the harder part. Now that they were inside, time was of the essence. They had no way of knowing whether or not Security Central had a system of checking with the guards at the gate every so often. If the head of Rimskor's security system did check them, he'd find them unconscious—at which point, the general alarm would be sounded all over the mountain. Speed, therefore, was the d'Alemberts' watchword.

Stun-guns at the ready and set on five, the invaders raced through the underground parking lot toward the elevator tube that was their destination. Instead of going to the first level, however, which included the ballroom and the main hall, they went up to the fourth level. According to Marcel's map, this was a level of auxiliary bedrooms and guest quarters. It was expected to be practically deserted at this time of night with no official functions going on in the castle, so the assault party would not have to worry about accidentally running into anyone who could sound the alarm. Plus, Marcel thought he had seen an entrance to the "forbidden area" on this level.

The hallway was dark, but that was only a minor inconvenience. Removing their gas masks, the team donned instead sets of infrared goggles and lights, so that they could make their way through the darkness. The special flashlights gave the entire corridor an eerie glow that accented the highly spartan decor; the place seemed even more bizarre than it did in normal light.

The floor was of highly polished metal, but even so the quartet of invaders made no noise at all as they moved quickly across it. Their special soft-soled sure-grip shoes muffled the sounds of their steps as they hurried across the floor. Their jumpsuits clung tightly to their bodies and didn't even rustle when they moved. They dared not make any sound that would alert the fortress's security patrol.

They found the desired doorway down the third hallway, right where Marcel had promised it would be. This area was as dark as the rest, and Luise knew she would never be able to work as efficiently as possible on the alarms while using only the infrared. Therefore, she switched on a small wheatgrain bulb of regular light and took off her goggles. Her comrades fanned out around her, keeping their goggles on and watching for any sign that might indicate the approach of a guard.

Taking out a handful of electronic sensors, Luise studied the alarm system built into this door. As Etienne had indicated, it was a fairly standard system; Duke Fyodor was obviously counting on the fact that it would be next to impossible for anyone to get this far. But of course, he didn't know about the d'Alemberts.

Luise had done a lot of studying in the field of electronics, and bypassing this alarm circuit was almost too easy. Once that was done, she picked the lock on the door and turned off her wheatgrain bulb, switching back to the infrared. Slowly she opened the door and led the way into the darkness beyond, with the other three following her.

She found herself standing on a narrow staircase leading downward. Her portable sensors scanned the steps carefully but found no sign of any alarms or pressure-sensitive plates that would alert the castle's forces to the presence of the intruders. She moved down the stairs as quickly as she could, always cautious of the way before her. She estimated she'd gone down two levels before she reached a landing and found a door on her left that would lead into the hidden portion of the castle.

A quick check showed that this door was not booby-trapped in any way; obviously this far into the inner sanctum the Duke was not concerned with oversecurity. He couldn't have his own people inadvertently setting off the alarms every time they opened a door. Luise relaxed. Except for one or two specially controlled areas, they wouldn't have to worry about tripping any warning devices.

Of course, it was just those specially controlled areas that they had to find; not much would be learned from an area where no secrets were kept.

The assault team went through the door and found themselves in a laboratory of some sort. After ascertaining that the place was empty except for themselves, they searched for and found the light switch. Instantly their eyes were dazzled by the brilliance after so long a period in darkness and the eerie glow of infrared, and it was almost a full minute before they were able to see again.

The workroom here was small—it was obviously a place for assembling microelectronic circuitry. The tools on the workbench—microscopes, jeweler's equipment, printboard for microcircuitry—were evidence of intent. Over to the side of the room, a glass wall separated this room from the next. A set of waldo controls manipulated a series of intricate devices on the other side. There was a metal slab that reminded Luise of nothing so much as an operating table, but it was bare at the moment, and there was no indication of what had been constructed on it.

Luise and her party combed the room quickly and thoroughly. There were a couple of scraps of notepaper on the desk top with long formulae and cryptic notations on them. The writing made no sense to Luise, but she slipped them into her pouch anyway; they might be significant to someone else.

When they had scoured the place completely and could find nothing else of value, they turned out the light and moved on through a door to the room beyond. This one was also small, empty, and dark—and much more disappointing. When they turned the light on, all they found was a couple of well-upholstered, comfortable chairs and a telecom machine on whose screen no messages were currently displayed. This room was even less informative than the first, so, with regret, the team moved on still further.

The next chamber they found held a surprise for them: pieces of skin lay scattered all over the floor, amid opened packing crates and small scraps of metal. On closer examination, though, the "skin" turned out to be a material called plastiderm—a substance widely used in the manufacture of prosthetics. All the d'Alemberts were familiar with it because the Duke's right hand was made from the substance. It looked and felt exactly like real skin when heated up to the proper temperature; at room temperature, though, it tended to be a bit stiffer and more brittle.

"From what I'm told," Luise whispered, "Duke Fyodor is a walking junkyard. He may need a lot of prosthetics to keep him going. This whole area may be nothing more than the area where his doctor works to keep him alive." Nevertheless, having no better leads, they decided to press onward.

The next room seemed to confirm Luise's guess. It was a comfortable study, with a desk and several padded chairs, plus three walls full of bookreels. Looking at titles at random, Luise could see that they were on biomechanics, prosthetics, organ transplants, artificial intelligence, and computer programming. Those last two puzzled her a little. She could understand that those first subjects would be needed to keep Duke Fyodor's body alive; but what would a surgeon need to know about artificial intelligence and computer programming? Surely the Duke had a brain of his own. Or could he be suffering from a disease that gradually destroyed the brain as well as the body, and was his doctor augmenting his mind with electronic aids? The situation did not make a whole lot of sense to her at the time, so she just filed the information away for later use.

There was no other way out of this study, and no other doors had been apparent in the chain of rooms that they'd gone through. They had come to the end of the line. There might well be more rooms in this hidden section of Rimskor Castle, but they would have to go out and find another way in if they were to reach them. Feeling very discouraged at their inability to learn anything incriminating against Duke Fyodor, Luise began leading her troops back out the way they'd come.

Suddenly the world exploded with alarm bells, and all the d'Alemberts were instantly ready for action. As far as Luise knew, they hadn't tripped any alarms, so the security forces wouldn't know precisely where in the castle they were. But perhaps the unconscious guards had been found at the front gate, or some other sign of the intrusion had been detected.

One thing, at any rate, was clear: they were going to have one hell of a time fighting their way out of this place—and they had not yet learned a single important fact!

Chapter 9

Encounter in the Dark

Borov's death, coming in such a manner, produced an instant chill throughout the members of the Progress. The rest of the ball was instantly canceled, and the fate of the next day's activities was in doubt as well. No one knew quite what to think; a million unanswered questions were floating around in everyone's mind, and no solutions were forthcoming. Jules and Jacques lifted the tree off Borov, and the body was taken off to the local hospital to have an autopsy performed. Yvette spent some time just staring at the tree, then wandered around the garden for a bit, her keen eyes observing everything in minute detail. Then most people went up to their rooms and prepared for bed.

Yvette went back to Edna and filled her in on what had happened. Then she and Yvonne took the Princess upstairs to her room, checked it out to make certain that no bombs had been placed there while they were out, and put the heiress to the Throne to bed with assurances that everything would be taken care of. Edna didn't believe the assurances any more than they did, but she pretended to so that the two women could get back to their real job—finding the traitor.

The four DesPlainians met secretly in Jules's room. It was the first opportunity they'd all had to talk together since coming to Cambria, but all of them were stunned by the events of the night and at first their air was so thick with worry that they found it hard to talk. Even the first kiss between Jules and Yvonne, who had been working so hard at not knowing each other for these past few days, was less than the passionate affair it normally would have been. Each was weighed down with preoccupation over the mystery of what had occurred.

Jacques and Yvette watched awkwardly as the two lovers kissed. Yvette knew that Jacques harbored an infatuation for her, one which she really did not return. They had been close friends since childhood, but that was all they ever could be as far as she was concerned. She could feel his pain as he watched his sister caress her brother and then as he turned his gaze to her. She could feel sorry for him—but pity was not love.

When Jules and Yvonne finished their embrace, Yvonne sat down on the edge of the bed, with Yvette beside her. Jacques sat on a chair in one corner. Jules, as was his wont, paced the room nervously. He always claimed to think better when he was on his feet and moving around.

By unspoken consent, Jules became the chairman of their meeting. "This is something none of us expected," he began with an understatement. "Something is happening here beyond our calculations, and we have to figure out what—and fast. Anyone care to offer a gut reaction?"

"Mine isn't very nice, I'm afraid," Yvette said, "but I'm not the slightest bit sorry that Borov is dead."

"He was a loud-mouthed bastard," Jacques agreed.

"But he was also our prime suspect," Jules said. "He came from Kolokov, where we got our initial lead about the time bomb. He was the one most determined to cause trouble for everyone else. With him out of the picture, everyone else is an equal suspect, and we're right back at word one."

"Maybe he was the traitor after all." That suggestion came from Vonnie. "Maybe he was coming back into the castle to plant the bomb when that tree fell on him."

Yvette shook her head. "Trees just don't fall over like that in a garden as well tended as this one is. Borov was murdered."

"Are you sure of that?" Jules asked.

"Positive. I looked that tree over pretty thoroughly.

There's not a trace of rot in it anywhere, nothing that would make it fall over on its own accord. The root system seemed sound and healthy. I saw the hole that tree came out of; it seemed to have been uprooted in one massive heave, because dirt was sprayed around the hole for a good distance around."

"Uprooted?" Jules knitted his brow in perplexity.

"You heard me right. My first thought was that someone must have chopped that tree down, or beamed it with a blaster—but there are no axe marks or burn marks on it anywhere and the entire trunk, from top to roots, is intact. It was pulled up out of its hole."

"But . . ." Jacques's voice trailed off as he contemplated that possibility. "But nobody's that strong. Didn't you see, it took Jules and me together to lift that tree off the body. Two DesPlainians, and that was only to shove the trunk over to one side. It would have taken a crane to lift that tree out of the ground and hit Borov with it."

"Maybe they had a crane," Yvonne suggested.

"Or a team of men," Yvette chimed in.

"Absolutely impossible. Remember, I had ordered the rest of the bodyguards and myself to be extra alert so that Borov wouldn't sneak in. We failed at that, obviously, but even so we couldn't have missed the sound of a crane or of three or four men working together crashing through the underbrush."

"We're getting a little far afield," Jules said, trying to soothe Jacques's ruffled feathers. "I agree with Jacques; there's no way a crane could have been brought in without alerting every guard on the estate. And as for the team hypothesis—I don't think there would be any group of men who, when they see they outnumber their opponent three or more to one, would think of uprooting a tree and dropping it on him. There are plenty of easier, faster, and more efficient ways of killing someone."

"We're getting away from our prime question," Yvette said. "We know there's been a murder. For the moment we're stumped on how the murderer did it, so let's turn our attention to the principal topic: *who* did it?"

Jules looked around the room at his friends' faces as the silence descended. "Well, it seems there are no clear-cut suspects that jump instantly to mind. Nobody really liked Borov very much, so they all have an equal motivation.

Except that there were three people whom Borov threatened to kill—me, Symond, and Liu."

"I think we can rule you out for the time being," Yvette smiled at her brother.

"*Merci!* That leaves us with two people having slightly stronger grounds that anyone else."

"But Borov threatened them, not the other way around," Jacques protested. "That doesn't seem to make sense."

"But suppose," Vonnie said, "that Borov sneaked back onto the grounds with the intent of killing someone. Instead, his intended victim got him first."

"But then why go to all the trouble with the tree?" Jacques asked. "If Borov really had tried to kill him, it was a pure case of self-defense. There were plenty of witnesses to Borov's threat; no prosecutor in the Galaxy would bring a case like that to trial, under the circumstances."

"But Borov was unarmed—at least when we found him," Yvonne persisted. "If he did have any weapon, his killer took it away from him. It doesn't make a good case for self-defense if the person you're defending yourself against is unarmed."

It was Yvette's turn to comment. "But perhaps the killer is also our traitor. If that's true, then even if this were a legitimate case of self-defense he wouldn't want to get involved. The spotlight would be focused on him, questions would be asked. He couldn't afford that kind of notoriety. As far as he knows, no one is aware that he's here for a treasonous purpose. He doesn't know his mission has already been compromised. And he'd work like hell to keep anyone from even suspecting."

There was silence for a long minute. Then Jules said slowly, "*Tu as raison,* as always, sis." He had learned from long experience that Yvette's most casual hunches were usually more perceptive than most people's carefully thought out theories, and he always listened to them. "If nothing else, this incident has shown us one thing. Before now, we couldn't even be certain that there was a traitor here. We were operating on a very faint clue and a probability. Now we know. Someone in this castle is a murderer, and is using that murder to cover up some darker secret."

He paced some more across the floor before continuing. "We need a few more details. When exactly did this murder take place?" He looked over in Jacques's direction.

"It couldn't have been before the ball started," said the male member of the Roumenier team. "My crew of bodyguards searched the grounds thoroughly. There was no sign of any uprooted tree or dead body."

His sister nodded confirmation. "That's right, we would have spotted anything as obviously out of place as that."

"Bien," Jules said with a thoughtful nod. "That gives us about a two-hour time span between the start of the ball and the moment when the body was discovered. We'll have to check people's stories and see whose movements can't be accounted for during that time."

"And in the meantime," said Yvette, "we keep up our own covers, even if it means that we become suspects ourselves."

"Absolutely," her brother agreed. "Right now, the traitor still thinks no one's on to him. We can't let him suspect that we know anything, or he may panic and do something rash. It never pays to upset a man holding a live bomb."

The police came the next day to question everybody about the events of the previous evening. Also, because of the fact that the Crown Princess and a baron and baroness were involved, several representatives from the local office of the Service of the Empire were also present.

The coroner's report had brought to light at least one astonishing fact. Though the tree had done a considerable amount of damage to the body—and, in fact, had made it difficult for the team of specialists to learn much of anything—the coroner was able to determine that the cause of death had been a sharp blow to the neck that had completely shattered the spinal column and the bottom portion of the skull. It was not until after the deceased's death that the tree had fallen on the body.

To everyone except the d'Alemberts and the Roumeniers this came as a considerable shock—and even the four DesPlainians pretended to be as startled as the rest. No longer could anyone think of this as merely a bizarre and unfortunate accident; it was a clear-cut case of murder.

The police did not dwell on the peculiar aspects of the case—and the obvious strength of the killer in lifting and wielding the tree against Borov—and instead chose to question the members of the Progress, particularly as to

106

their whereabouts during the evening. They had determined the time of death to within half an hour—and it happened to be the half-hour that included the formal break in the ball's activity. Suddenly everyone was trying to remember what they did during that break, and not everyone was entirely successful.

Yvette had been talking to Edna during much of the break, and Jules had been discreetly carrying on a friendly conversation with Yvonne. Most of the candidates had gone outside into the garden with some of Edna's ladies-in-waiting, and so had built-in alibis for the crucial interval. Only three of the men did not have such alibis—Paul Symond, Choyen Liu, and a fellow named Sean Mulvaney from the planet Arcta. Mulvaney said that he had been visiting the fresher then, and had no witnesses to his activity. Symond said he had gone up to his room to get a couple of pieces of jewelry he had forgotten to bring down to the ball with him originally. Liu admitted that he had gone out into the garden by himself to meditate.

The police zeroed in on him. The fact that he had no alibi for the time in question, that he admitted being in the garden at that time, and that Borov had threatened him earlier in the day made him a prime suspect. Liu accepted that suspicion quietly, saying very little except to answer every question the police put to him. He stated politely but firmly that he did not murder Borov and that he did not know who did. Neither the operatives from SOTE nor the police detectives could make a dent in that story.

Finally, they had to give up. There was not yet enough evidence to make an arrest, or even to take any one person down to the police station for more detailed questioning. Since all the suspects were here for the Progress, which was to last for another week and a half, the police left them alone and went out instead to look over the garden and search for more clues. After a while, they departed completely, with the warning that no one in the Progress party was to leave the planet without checking with them first.

All the rest of the day the topic of conversation centered around the murder. Symond, Mulvaney, and Liu were made unofficial outcasts, with very few people bothering to talk to them or ask their opinions. Liu took this all with the same quiet acceptance he affected toward everything;

the other two were a bit more annoyed that their integrity should be so questioned, but they tried to exhibit good humor despite their awkward positions.

Midway through the day, Jules found an opportunity to take his sister aside and talk with her privately. "The thought has occurred to me," he said, "that we may have the number of the enemy figured all wrong. What if there are *two* traitors here—one to plant the bomb and the other to act as his backup? If there are more than one of them here, it might let those three off the hook; the killer would say he was elsewhere and his confederate would back his story."

Yvette mulled that over for a second. "You may be right," she said at last. "There simply aren't enough data to go by. Having only one infiltrator in this group would be simpler; remember how hard it is to qualify. But I suppose there could be more than one."

"We'll just have to generate more data, then," Jules said resolutely. "And I think I know how to do it. I'll drop a little bomb of my own."

He waited until dinnertime to do it, though. While everyone was seated around the large banquet table—talking about the murder, naturally—Jules suddenly dropped into the conversation the fact that he had a pretty good idea who the murderer was. Edna gave him a strange glance, wondering what sort of game he was playing, but, like the intelligent woman she was, she said nothing. Instead she left it to the others to ask questions that had formed in her mind as well.

There was no dearth of questioners. "Who is it?" asked Hans Gudding.

Jules shook his head. "I don't really want to say yet—except that it isn't me. But this is a serious charge, and I wouldn't want to slander anyone on just what evidence I have. If I turned out to be wrong, I would never forgive myself for calling an innocent man a killer."

"Shouldn't you tell the police about your suspicions?" Paul Symond asked.

"I probably should, once I get them firmed up a bit. Tomorrow morning, first thing, I'll give them a call and explain my theory."

"What exactly do you have?" Mulvaney asked.

"There've been several things that happened over the

few days we've all been together. The person I suspect has done a couple of things that struck me at the time as being most peculiar. There are one or two facts I want to check on out in the garden." As he had by now finished eating, he pushed his chair away from the table. "Please excuse me, all of you, but this could be important."

He left the room, much to everyone's surprise, and went outside to roam around the garden. He spent two hours alone out there, wandering the paths and occasionally bending over to examine something under the dim light of Ansegria's only moon. He spent a lot of time around the site where the body had been discovered, turning up rocks and walking around in circles. Occasionally people inside the house would stare out at him through the windows, wondering what he expected to find, but they preferred not to know. They let him wander by himself.

That suited Jules just perfectly, for what he was hoping to find would not be in the garden at all.

Finally, when the hour was getting quite late, Jules decided to return to the castle. Most of the people, he discovered, had already retired for the evening; though they had done very little today compared to the other days, the psychological toll the murder had taken on all of them was enormous. Finding almost no one to talk to, Jules decided to head up to his own room as well.

As Jules turned into the hallway that led to his own room, he noticed that the light was out, leaving the entire corridor in pitch blackness. The instant that fact registered in his mind, he leaped into action—literally. Pushing off with his powerful leg muscles, he dived forward and to his right, curling himself into a tight ball and rolling until he bumped into the wall on that side.

His action was well taken. Even as he jumped, the low buzzing sound of a stun-gun carried through the air. Its beam passed just centimeters to the side of where he was, although he had no way of knowing just how close it came. All he had known was that, standing in the light in front of a darkened area, he made the perfect target silhouette for anyone wanting to shoot at him, and he had taken the appropriate action to neutralize that.

Now that he was in motion he stood a much better chance of surviving. The odds against him would be determined by the skill and reflexes of his attacker—unknown factors, but Jules was not too worried. His DesPlainian reflexes were sure to be better than those of a normal human.

The movement of his roll against the wall brought him to his feet in a low crouch. Without pausing as much as a split second, he leaped again—mostly forward this time and only slightly to his left. He was pretty certain he knew where his attacker would be positioned—at the very back of the darkened corridor, where he could see Jules's silhouette approaching all the time . . . and where Jules would not be able to see him. By constantly moving toward his enemy, Jules would be narrowing the distance between them as well as shortening the man's reaction time. All he had to do was avoid making his leaps in any consistent pattern and he should be all right.

Again, the buzzing sound of the stunner beam was heard, at shorter and shorter intervals. A stun-gun could not be set on continuous fire as could a blaster, and needed a fraction of a second between bursts for it to recharge. That was what Jules was counting on most; if his opponent had been using a blaster, Jules would have had to retreat, since he couldn't have reached his quarry before the deadly beam sliced a hole through his DesPlainian body.

Using a series of leap, roll, leap again motions, Jules made his way down the blacked out corridor toward his foe. The buzzing of the stunner took on an almost desperate whine as the traitor fired repeatedly to rid himself of this upstart who was unexpectedly fast. Jules, too, was a little surprised at how close together the shots were; his opponent must have lightning quick reflexes himself, and that was a sobering thought. He hadn't supposed any of the other members of the Progress were quite that good.

But there was no time to ponder that; all he could do was file it in his memory for future use. At present, he was too busy with the problem of staying alive.

He knew the length of the hallway and could estimate his leaps pretty well. In three more jumps he was near the end, and should be within range of his opponent. They were both theoretically at a disadvantage now, since both were in equal darkness and neither could see the other's silhouette. Jules flailed out in the most likely direction where his antagonist would be, expecting the other's blows to be just as uncertain.

Instead, a powerful fist came flying through the air at

110

him, catching him squarely under the jaw. Had he really been, as he claimed, from the mythical planet Julea with its standard one-gee gravity, the blow would undoubtedly have knocked him unconscious and possibly broken his jaw as well. But Jules was from DesPlaines, with a gravity three times Earth's normal, and his family had lived on that tough, rockbound world for over four centuries. They had adapted to life under such harsh conditions; their bones were heavier, their muscles tighter, their reflexes faster than those of people from more reasonable planets. Added to that heritage was Jules's circus training and superb physical conditioning. He and his sister were, to quote the Head of the Service, "the two most capable people alive."

Consequently, the blow was not as disabling as it was intended to be. Jules was caught by surprise at its accuracy and knocked downward, but he possessed both the mental and physical agility to roll with the punch. As he fell backward, he brought one foot up and delivered a vicious blow to the spot where his enemy's ribcage would have to be.

He could feel the blow connect solidly, could feel his foot driving into the other man's chest. That kick should have shattered the opponent's ribs, possibly puncturing the heart or a lung. At the very least, it should have doubled his antagonist over with pain and left him gasping for breath, helpless against any further action Jules cared to take.

It did none of those things. Instead, all it did was push him backwards and keep him slightly off balance for a couple of seconds.

They were a crucial couple of seconds, though, for Jules had to regain his own balance; had the blow not been delivered the SOTE agent would have been an open target for the other man's stun-gun. As it was, Jules's head was ringing from the force of the traitor's punch. He fell, rolled, and staggered to his feet slower than he optimally would have. The strength of the other's blow and the ineffectiveness of his own stunned him.

His only hope lay in keeping himself in motion, keeping his superbody pounding out an attack against this mysterious assailant. *Don't give him time to get off a shot* was the rule of the moment; at such short range the man could hardly miss.

Fortunately, the hallway was not too wide. Jules knew the man would have moved slightly out of his previous position, but he wouldn't have been able to move far if he wanted to keep Jules between himself and the light at the other end of the corridor. Jules lunged at a spot where he guessed the man would be, and felt his own hand connect solidly with the other's flesh. At the same time, though, he felt a strong chopping blow to his own side. The traitor seemed to know exactly where to aim, whereas Jules was literally stabbing in the dark.

Suddenly the air was filled with the sound of a familiar voice calling, "Rube!" The abbreviated circus cry of danger had survived to this present day, and could be coming from only one other person on this entire planet—his sister, Yvette. Even as the pain in his side made him double over, Jules felt a slight cheering in his soul. Together, the two DesPlainians made a team that no one in the Universe could stop.

Yvette, even though her eyes were not accustomed to the darkness, could tell where the fighting was by the sounds of the action. Like a fury on wheels, she waded into the battle with both hands whirling like the vanes of a windmill. She had charged straight into combat without having to dodge stunner beams, and so hers was a much more frontal assault. As fast as she moved, though, the traitor seemed to know, despite the darkness, where she was going to swing and was able to block each blow with the appropriate countermeasure.

Although none of Yvette's punches landed solidly, they did keep the enemy busy fending them off. Meanwhile, Jules had recovered his breath from the blow to his ribs and was beginning to enter the fray again on his own. He had to be careful in the darkness not to hit his sister instead of their common enemy; but even so, they had worked together as a team for so long that their reactions and their timing were almost instinctive. As Yvette's hand would be drawing back to deliver another blow, Jules's fist would be striking out at their opponent; and vice versa, of course. The two d'Alemberts had worked for years in a circus act where their very lives depended on the precise timing of their cooperation, and such training was hard to lose.

No mortal man could ever have survived such an onslaught of power and fury—yet, the traitor was at least able to hold his own in this ferocious battle. While he was no longer able to assume the offensive, he could still manage to block every single one of their blows with speed of reflex that rivalled—or even surpassed—their own.

Finally, though, the antagonist realized how futile this fighting was. His whole strategy had been to do this deed quickly and then get away, before anyone could discover him. The trio of fighters could now well be deadlocked for another five minutes, the way this battle was going—by which time, other people were bound to come along and discover him. He dared not let his anonymity be stripped from him, even at the cost of letting these two people live.

Thus, with one gargantuan effort, he reached through the defenses of the two d'Alemberts and grabbed each of them by the front of their shirts. Before even their superfast reflexes could react, he had picked them both up bodily and flung them against the corridor's left-hand wall. Both agents had the wind knocked out of them as they bounced against the wall and each other and rebounded onto the floor. They recovered their senses and looked around, but it was too late. They could hear the sound of the traitor's footsteps racing down the hallway, at a speed equal to at least anything they could do. They caught a quick glimpse of a male figure silhouetted against the light at the far end of the corridor, and then that vanished as their foe turned the corner and fled into other sections of the castle. By the time they had righted themselves on their feet, they knew there would be no chance of catching up with their elusive antagonist.

Yvette reached out to steady her brother, who seemed a bit more wobbly on his feet than she was. "All smooth?" she asked.

"I think so. I'm sure glad you happened along."

"Well, you baited the trap so nicely, I just thought I'd drop by to see what you caught. As you suspected, whoever it was wanted to silence you before you could talk to the police."

Jules shook his head ruefully. "Yeah. It almost worked too well."

He was considerably worried. This fight in the hallway had shown them a number of startling facts about their opponent. He had amazingly quick reflexes. He could move

113

with a speed that made even them look like slowpokes. He could see in the dark. He could absorb blows that would kill or cripple any ordinary human being.

And, as had already been shown, he could uproot a tree and drop it on someone—a tree that it took two DesPlainians just to lift.

What sort of man was it they were fighting?

Chapter 10

The Dumbwaiter Express

When the alarms went off all over Rimskor Castle, the four d'Alembert intruders, who had already been moving fast, became a blur of activity. To hesitate even the slightest now would mean certain capture and possible death.

Luise was in charge, and she thought with lightning speed. They were in the blocked-off area, which had turned out to be a cul-de-sac. They could not allow themselves to be discovered here, or they'd be easily trapped. Leading the way, she raced out of the medical office, through the supply room, the teletype room, and the laboratory. With her three relatives behind her, she bounded up the stairs six at a time, and did not hesitate until she reached the top. Even then she paused only long enough to draw her stunner before bursting out the door into the hallway.

They were in luck—the hall was still deserted. How long that luck would last was another matter, however, because there were certain to be servants, security guards, or robots checking up on this floor any second. And all the elevator tubes would now be guarded, so they could not be used to go between floors.

To make matters worse, Luise knew they could not leave. The front gate—and only way out of the castle—would now be so heavily guarded that even four top-notch agents like these d'Alemberts could not fight their way out. To even attempt to leave without having learned anything would be an admission of failure—a fate truly worse than death to these members of the Galaxy's most talented clan.

Luise raced down the darkened corridor toward a place that Marcel had tentatively marked on his map as a stairway. It, too, would be guarded, of course—but less so, and her team would have more room for maneuvering on a stairway than in an elevator tube.

Just as she reached the stairway, the door to it opened in her face and a robot guard started to come through. It was hard to say who was more startled, Luise or the robot, but it is a fact that Luise reacted first. She automatically fired the stunner point blank into the creature, even as her mind was telling her reflexes that a stun-gun would have no effect on a robot.

The machine was an upright cylinder, only a meter and a half high, with a dozen metal tentacles ringed around its body to act as limbs. One of those tentacles currently held a stun-gun of its own, and was bringing it quickly into a firing position. While Luise's stunner would not affect the robot, its stunner *would* affect her—unless she took steps to avoid it immediately.

Reaching out with her left hand, Luise grabbed the robot by the tentacle that held the gun and pulled it toward her. The machine massed close to a hundred kilograms, but even so the strength of her tug pulled it off its balance. With the power of a person born on a three-gee world, and the expertise that only a d'Alembert could achieve, she whipped the bulky contrivance around her and spun it further into the hallway.

Rick took up where she left off. As the robot came past him, he grabbed it and lifted it bodily off the ground. The big wrestler hefted it as though it were a feather pillow, holding it high above his head for a second and then flinging it against the nearest wall. The robot hit with a crash that threatened to shatter their eardrums and fell to the floor, a pile of useless scrap metal. A few sparks hissed and fizzed inside its cylindrical body, but it was incapable of further action.

The problem was that Luise couldn't be sure whether the robot was acting on its own or whether it was linked via some control circuit to a master console. If the latter were the case, they had just given their position completely away; even now an army of similar robots might be descending on them from all the other levels of the castle.

She went into the stairwell from which the robot had

116

come and looked up and down. The lower levels of the castle would be the more heavily guarded, since any intruders would have to go that way eventually to get out, and that was the direction in which any sensible person would head. Luise's first thought, then, was to go upward, to play for time and position, to make the game last as long as possible and hope to take advantage of some break in her favor. She and her team did start upward, but they only got up one flight before they heard the sounds of a whole legion of metal feet on the stairs above them. She did not want to face a squad of killer robots if she could possibly help it.

Reluctantly, then, she turned her team around and started them back down the stairs. They moved at top speed, easily outdistancing the machines behind them. There was no opposition as they continued to descend, until finally the stairs came to an end at the ground level and they faced another door opening outward. With the army of robots behind them, they had no choice but to go out that door and risk whatever might be facing them. Before they did that, though, they put away their stun-guns and took out their blasters instead. From everything Etienne had told them about Duke Fyodor, the lord of Rimskor Castle had a much greater fondness for machines than for people, and the great majority of his security force was likely to be robots. Stunners would be worse than useless against such antagonists.

The stairs entered out into a long hallway, one much fancier than the upstairs bedroom corridor. This one was decorated with metal sculptures both realistic and surrealistic. Platinum gargoyles up in the corners of the ceiling leered down at them, and the smooth floor could provide treacherous footing.

The scene in the hallway was pandemonium. Humans and robots alike were scurrying back and forth in confusion at the mere thought of an unprecedented break-in to this stronghold. The sudden appearance of four silver-clad furies only added to their confusion—and Luise was only too glad to take advantage of that fact.

Four blaster beams rayed out at once, slicing down everyone—human or robot—in the corridor. Luise glanced both ways down the hall and saw no one else coming immediately. Her trouble was that she was as lost as anyone, now. The running around, the flights up and down stairs, had disoriented a mind even as sharp as hers was. She had no idea where this corridor was in relation to the map Marcel had shown her, and until she could find some familiar territory they would just have to take their chances and wander aimlessly.

Which was not to say slowly. Although she didn't know herself where she was going, Luise didn't hesitate to run to her right, with the other three still following behind her. They came to what had to be the kitchen, and she could regain her bearings now—and curse her luck. She had chosen the wrong direction, and they were in the back of the house. They would now have to fight their way all the way to the front of the castle if they wanted to have any chance at all of escaping. Yet such a fight—through the entire line of Duke Fyodor's guards—would be tantamount to suicide.

Luise looked wildly around for another alternative, and her eyes fell on the dumbwaiter system. According to what Etienne had told her, this series of mechanized tubeways ran all through the castle, with exits to virtually every room. The tunnels were small and cramped but, with the exception of Rick, all the d'Alemberts were relatively small themselves. If the invaders could squeeze themselves through this system, they would be like mice in the walls, going where they wanted at will.

The only problem was that the Duke's defenders could track them to this kitchen, and from there it would be a simple matter to deduce where the intruders had gone. Luise was faced with a hard executive decision—but she did not shirk it. "Rick," she said, "we have to go through the dumbwaiter. It's our only way. But they'll know we've gone in there and can flush us out unless at least one of us is left outside causing them confusion."

"Don't worry," Rick said, eyeing the dumbwaiter 'entrance. "It looks a little small for me, anyway. I'll give them so much hell they'll think all four of us are still on the loose."

Luise flashed her relative a quick smile. The d'Alembert family loyalty was such that any of them would have done the same for the others had the situation warranted. Rick was the logical choice in this situation.

Then, without wasting any more time, Luise ran over to

the entrance and lay down on the conveyor belt that fed into the hole in the wall. The belt was not turned on at the present time, which meant she had to crawl forward—but she was still safe from discovery for the moment. Behind her, Jeanne and Claude also inched their way into the tubes.

Thus began more than an hour of nightmare for the Circus trio as they crawled through the very foundations of Rimskor Castle itself. Luise tried to keep them headed in the general direction of the front of the building, though the tubeway took so many right-angle turns that it was hard to keep the direction straight. Twice they had to change levels, climbing with difficulty up a series of grippers in the walls that were designed for holding packages. They passed occasional doors, but a peek out of them showed Luise that those rooms were well guarded and that to leave the dumbwaiter would be to invite certain death.

Occasionally, too, they could hear the sounds of fighting coming through the walls. True to his word, Rick d'Alembert was giving the defenders a hard time. Fighting against truly overwhelming odds, he was making his presence felt throughout the castle and keeping attention from being focused on the tubes where his comrades were installed. How he stayed alive, none of the other three could guess; but they all prayed that his luck would continue and trusted to his special skills as a d'Alembert.

Finally the trio came to another door that opened out into a room beyond. Sliding the door open just a tiny crack, Luise ventured a peek inside. There were only two robot guards in the room—the lowest number of any she had yet seen. There was one human, unarmed, and another thing that at first she took to be a tall machine until it turned and she could see that it was really Duke Fyodor, firmly enmeshed in the mechanical cradle that kept him alive. A board of flashing lights across the room gave some evidence that this might be the central nerve point for all the castle's security operations—in which case she had reached an unintended but quite welcome destination.

She whispered the news most quietly to her two companions and explained her plans. Then, scrunching herself up as best she could in the narrow tunnel, she prepared for action. When she was absolutely ready, she slid the door all the way open and kicked off against the back wall of the tube. Her beautiful, agile body sprang outward and sailed through the air into the security office, completely startling the four occupants.

Before anyone had a chance to react, Luise had hit the ground, rolled, and come up with her blaster at the ready. The two robot guards were just a fraction of a second too slow as the SOTE agent's beam cut each of them in two. As the other d'Alemberts began scrambling out of the dumbwaiter, Luise trained her weapon on the two humans. "Don't try anything," she warned—superfluously, for the Duke and his associate were not about to make any foolish moves while staring down the muzzle of a blaster.

As soon as Jeanne and Claude were both safely inside the room, Luise turned her thoughts to Rick, possibly still out there fighting for his life. "I want you to call your guards and tell them to stop fighting at once. One of my friends is still out there."

"He's already been stunned down," the Duke said morosely. "We were just about to go question him when you arrived." He paused to regather his strength and assume an air of outraged dignity. "I hope you realize that, whoever you are and whatever you think you're accomplishing by this raid, it will never work. I am duke of this entire planet, and I won't rest until you're tracked down and destroyed."

Luise paid no attention to his bravado. Instead, she waited until both Claude and Jeanne had drawn their own stunners, then tucked her weapon inside her belt. Reaching into her utility pouch, she pulled out a small hyposprayer filled with a colorless liquid. "This," she said without emotion, "is nitrobarb. You've heard of it, of course, and you know what it can do. You have a few answers that I need, and I intend to get them."

The Duke had indeed heard of nitrobarb. He knew that it had a 50 percent mortality rate on healthy people, and he knew that, if he survived the drug itself, he would never survive the repercussions of the answers he would reveal under its influence. "This is highly illegal," he protested.

Luise stared at him coldly. "So is treason, Your Grace, and that's what we're talking about, isn't it?"

As Luise took a step toward the ruler of Kolokov, the other prisoner in the room spoke up. "Please, don't give

120

him that injection. The Duke is a very weak man, his system couldn't tolerate it. As his doctor, I can tell you he'd be dead in minutes and you wouldn't learn a thing.

Luise turned to look at him. "You must be Doctor Rustin, then." She paused to consider his words. It was well known that Duke Fyodor had lived on the edge of death since childhood. The very fact that his body was only kept alive by carting around such an incredible contraption testified to its frailty. Nitrobarb *was* very strong, and what the doctor said could very well be true. She could be murdering a duke to absolutely no gain.

But what choice had she? Her mission here was a failure unless she could discover some more about the time bomb that was to be used against the Princess. No other questioning would be effective, either, for the Duke could lie under less strenuous procedures.

She had to follow through on her bluff and hope to crack something. "Well, doctor," she continued, "the penalty for high treason is death, anyway. What does it matter whether it comes sooner or later?" She took another step toward the Duke.

Duke Fyodor's skin was normally quite pale, and his system would not let him sweat. But if those two conditions had not been true, he would have been ashen and perspiring. He had lived close to death as long as he could remember. His earliest recollections were of hospitals and sickrooms and doctors with funereal expressions. It had scared him, that thought of crossing into the unknown, and he had fought back with everything at his disposal. And he had won. He had fought death and conquered it; even if it made him look like a freak, even if he were despised, he had won and he had lived. And he was not going to let someone kill him now, even if it meant betraying his best friend.

"Him!" he shouted, pointing at Dr. Rustin. "Do it to him. He knows as much as I do, he was in on all of it. He made it work."

Luise stopped, rather bemused that her bluff had paid off. Dr. Rustin was well known as the Duke's constant companion. It did make sense that he would have been his partner in treachery as well. "I suppose it's worth a try," she said aloud. "But if I don't get any answers from him, I can still try you next."

121

Dr. Rustin cowered as she came near him. He was, after all, an older man and the nitrobarb could well kill him, too, though he was in good health for his age. But he had no choice and in only a few minutes he was in a stupor that would last for twenty minutes—the first stage of the drug's effects.

During that interval, the room was as quiet as a grave-yard at midnight. Duke Fyodor, still in fright at this threat to his continued existence, sat limply in one corner and wondered where he had gone wrong. The three d'Alem-berts did not converse among themselves; the situation was too critical, and they did not want to make any slip-ups that might give away their identities.

Finally, Dr. Rustin began showing signs of coming around. His eyes opened, but were glazed over in an ex-pression that showed the extent of his drugged state. Luise sat down opposite him and questioned him firmly.

"You and Duke Fyodor have plotted treason against the Empire, haven't you?" she asked sternly.

"Yes," was the slow, stupefied answer.

Despite herself, Luise let out a sigh of relief. All this while there had been the nagging fear in the back of her mind that perhaps she and her family were wrong, that they were taking all this hostile action against innocent parties. Now that fear was banished forever, and she could continue on with her interrogation. "Did you hire Rawl Winsted to help you?"

"Yes."

"Why did you need his help?"

"He was good at working with the small parts of the robot."

Robot? Luise knit her brow in perplexity. "I thought you were making a time bomb."

A low, droning sound came out of Rustin's mouth. Luise had made a statement, not a direct question, and his drugged mind could not completely cope with it. She mentally cursed herself for sloppy technique and rephrased her last utterance.

"What sort of a robot were you making?"

"One that looked and acted exactly like a human being."

Where is all this leading? she wondered. What was the connection between a time bomb and a robot? "Did you ever use the phrase 'time bomb' in Winsted's presence?"

"Yes."

"What was the context?" Luise was getting frustrated by the short, pointed answers. That was the main problem with interrogation by nitrobarb—it left the interviewee totally without will and not capable of involved thought.

"I said that the robot would be a time bomb against the Princess and the Imperial Family."

"What made you think that?"

"Because it was going to marry Princess Edna and would be her husband while she was on the Throne."

Pieces suddenly began falling into place. A robot that looked and acted exactly like a human being. It would go on the Progress and the Princess would meet it. "But how could you be so sure the Princess would want to marry it?"

"It was programmed to like everything she liked and to conform to her ideals of the perfect husband."

A chill went down Luise's spine. This was the most insidious plan she had ever heard of. It sounded crazy; no one could have so much information about the Princess as to design her perfect mate for her. And yet, there were computer mating services that did have astonishing success records. And if this were true, it would have far more impact on the fate of the Empire than a mere bomb. There were, after all, other legitimate, if indirect, heirs in the Succession if anything should happen to Edna; but having a husband who was privy to all the secrets of the Empire and who could advise in ways that might lead to her eventual downfall would have much more far-reaching and potentially dangerous consequences for the fate of the Galaxy.

"How can you be so sure that this robot wouldn't be spotted as a fraud at once?"

"None of the others has."

If the previous answer gave Luise a chill, this one froze her completely. "Do you mean that you've made other robots who are masquerading as human beings?"

"Yes."

"Were they all supposed to marry the Princess?"

"No, they had a variety of missions."

"How many of them are there, what are their names, what are their purposes, how long have they been in existence, have any of them been successful?"

Luise was so flabbergasted by this revelation that she

could not stop the questions from gushing forth. This could be one of the most important—and unexpected—breakthroughs SOTE had ever made. For the security of the Galaxy, those questions had to be answered.

Dr. Rustin's jaws moved, but no intelligible sounds came forth. His drugged mind could only work on one item at a time, and Luise had bombarded him with so many things that he didn't know where to begin. He sat staring fixedly ahead, his poor confused mind running in circles.

While all eyes in the room had been on the doctor, Duke Fyodor saw an opportunity to make his move. He had edged closer to the control board, where he kept a stungun under the console. Now, when the attention of everyone else in the room was hanging on Rustin's words, he acted.

Reaching quickly under the table, he pulled out his gun and fired. The weapon was set on ten—instantly lethal, and his target fell to the floor, dead. Dr. Rustin would betray no more of the secrets on which he and the Duke had worked for so many years.

Claude spotted the Duke's motion and fired his own stunner, but just an instant too late to prevent Rustin's death. As the ray hit Duke Fyodor, his entire body went through a series of convulsions like a full epileptic seizure. He thrashed wildly about, and fell with a heavy crash into the control console. There was an eruption of sparks and the Duke screamed, then lay very still.

Luise ran over to him, but she was too late. The man who had ruled Kolokov was dead. "What setting was your stunner on?" she demanded of Claude. She had wanted the Duke kept alive, if possible.

"I'd reset it for three," he said, bewildered. "It should only have knocked him out for half an hour."

"He was unnatural anyway," said Jeanne, who had not volunteered her opinion since this mission began. "There was a wrongness in him. It reacted badly to the beam, I think."

Luise looked at Jeanne and could see the girl trembling. This entire experience had been a bad one for her, though she had borne it without complaint because it was her duty. The animal trainer was a sensitive, and in tune with living things; being surrounded by so many mechanical menaces was playing hell on her nerves.

"Well, whatever the case, we have enough information for SOTE to act on."

"If we can get it out of here," Claude said.

Luise took a small metal box out of her pouch. It was a radio bleeper, and the signal it sent out would inform Duke Etienne that they had gotten what they needed. The Circus manager would be stationed near Rimskor Castle with an army of SOTE agents, waiting for that signal to invade in force. Luise pressed the button and a red light went on, indicating that the bleeper was sending out its signal.

She waited a minute for the green light beside the red one to light up as well, an acknowledgement that the Duke had received her signal. The green light did not go on.

"What's the matter?" Claude asked, reading the puzzled expression on her face.

"Our signal's not getting out. We can't reach them." Luise looked over at the control board. "Maybe it can't get through the metal sides of the mountain. Or maybe there's something jamming outbound transmission."

"What do we do, then?"

What indeed? They were a long way from the gate, and the castle was still crawling with guards and booby traps. Their number was already reduced by one, as Rick lay somewhere either stunned or in captivity—or dead. The only two men who could have neutralized the defenses had both been killed—and now Luise, Claude, and Jeanne were the only three people living who knew this information. They would have been willing, before, to die for their cause. Now they had to live to get the information to SOTE.

But how?

Chapter 11

Bur-Bur to the Rescue

"You don't suppose," Luise said slowly to her comrades, "that Duke Fyodor would have left his communicator lines open?"

"Not if he's gone to all the trouble to blank out internal radio communication," Claude said. "At least, I wouldn't. I'd want to make sure that if anyone did manage to get in, they wouldn't get out again—nor would any information that they had learned. Once my security network was in place, I'd see to it that nothing got out until I wanted it to."

Luise grimaced. "That's what I was afraid of." She went over to the security control board and studied it for a few seconds; but nothing on it was labeled, and she could make no sense of it. "No way to figure out how to turn the alarms off or send out an all-clear," she sighed. "I'd be afraid of pushing the wrong button and blowing us all up. We're just going to have to fight our way out."

There were two alternatives open. The three of them

could split up and each try to find his way out separately, thus tripling the chances that at least one of them would make it outside alive with the vital information. Or, they could stay together to form a cohesive unit. They would all be grouped in one place, and one lucky strike could get them all; but a tightly knit band of d'Alemberts made an awfully invincible force. The opposition had been further weakened since their last run-in with them—Rick had done that much, although now he was out of action. Luise decided on the latter alternative, to keep them all together. Picking her blaster out of her belt once more, she said *"Eh bien,* let's go!"

The trio went storming out of the security room into the hallway. There were only two robot guards there, and neither had expected an attack to come from that direction. Both went down quickly under the d'Alemberts' beams, without having the slightest chance to sound the alarm.

There were only two other doorways in the corridor for them to try. Luise headed for the nearer one, flung the door open and darted through it . . . only to find herself standing on one of the ramps in the Chamber of Angles that Etienne had described. The ceiling vaulted high above her head, the crazy mobiles gleamed as they reflected the room's bright light, and the subsonic vibrations drilled into her bone and nerve tissues in a pattern designed to drive even the calmest of people to distraction. And in this situation, Luise was not the calmest of people.

Still, there were no defenders in the room at this moment and the ramp was a way for them to get down to the ground level. Luise started forward, her acrobatic shoes making almost no noise on the polished metal flooring. Behind her, she could tell that the room's craziness was affecting Jeanne even worse than it did her—but then, the teen-ager was the most sensitive member of the group. The poor girl was trembling like a leaf in a high wind as she was forced to traverse the coldly mechanical horror of this chamber—but again, she did it without complaint, because she was a d'Alembert.

They only made it halfway down the ramp before a party of robots wandered through the room and spotted them. The d'Alemberts' blasters fired quickly again, but not before one of the robots had managed to send out a high, piercing whistle that would bring an army of other guards running into the area.

The trio of invaders took cover behind the solid metal bannister of the ramp and waited for the attack on them to begin. It did not take long. Seemingly dozens of robots appeared in various doorway entrances to this chamber, all firing up at the intruders. Luise cautioned her companions not to waste their fire; the charge packs in their own blasters were getting low. They could only afford to fire when they had a sure shot.

Luise noticed out of the corner of her eye that Jeanne's shots were becoming more and more erratic as the eeriness of the room took its toll on her, and finally the young animal trainer stopped firing completely and curled up into a whimpering ball. Luise regretted having to take someone so young and inexperienced along on a mission like this, but her special talents had been deemed necessary to help them get through the outer gate.

Inside Jeanne's jumpsuit, Luise could see a stirring motion, indicating that Bur-Bur the ticklemouse was awake and restless. The subsonics were probably affecting him just as badly as they were hitting his mistress. Luise felt a twinge of pity for the helpless creature—then shut that feeling off abruptly as an idea occurred to her. Telling Claude to keep up the covering fire for all of them, she knelt down beside Jeanne and spoke rapidly.

"Can you still control Bur-Bur?" she asked.

It took a second for the question to sink into Jeanne's consciousness. The younger girl looked up and said, "I . . . I don't know. I think so, if it's nothing too complicated. Why?"

Luise reached into her pocket and pulled out the little transmitter. "He has more chance of getting past the guards and out of here than we do. We can strap this around his waist like we did with the tirascaline canister, and as soon as he runs outside the gate it should start transmitting. Can you get him to do that?"

Jeanne nodded. *"Oui.* All his natural instincts are telling him to run now, anyway. I would only have to make sure he runs in the proper direction."

So saying, the animal trainer reached inside the front of her jumpsuit and took out her little pet. The animal was clearly skittish, and Jeanne had to take several seconds

128

looking it straight in the eyes and cooing to it gently—while blasterfire was raging all around them—to calm it down. Luise noted with relief that this effort was good therapy for Jeanne, too; with some definite goal in mind, she was snapping out of the panic that had so recently enveloped her.

Taking the bleeper now from Luise, Jeanne attached it to the saddle that was around Bur-Bur's middle. She spoke to the ticklemouse in low tones and in pseudowords that Louise couldn't begin to understand. It was fascinating to watch, even though they were in so much danger at the moment. Jeanne was able to put aside reality to reach down to the creature's level; she actually seemed to become a ticklemouse herself as she communicated her desires to Bur-Bur.

Finally she straightened up again. "He's ready," she said. "But there's so much shooting going on in here right now, I don't know if he'll even be able to get out of the room."

From over at the edge of the ramp, Claude spoke up. "Hand him to me," he said. "I'll take care of it." Obediently, Jeanne handed the still nervous pet to her comrade, who took it and tucked it gently inside his own jumpsuit. Then, with a simple "Cover me," he leaped, literally, into action.

Taking off from a crouched position, he used his powerful legs—born to a gravity three times as strong as this—to propel him upward over the banister into the air. With one arm outstretched, he reached for and grabbed the support strut of one of the multitudinous mobiles that were hanging throughout the room. Pushing off against that, he began a downward curve toward the door that led to the front of the castle. As he descended, his body twisted and spun so rapidly that it presented a very bad target to the defenders.

While he was in the air, Luise followed his last orders. The robot guards were not expecting a move like this, and momentarily were at a loss for what to do. When they finally decided to take aim, they concentrated solely on Claude and forgot all about the other two intruders. As they stepped out of their doorways to get a better shot at the acrobat, beams from Luise's and Jeanne's blasters cut them down, decimating their ranks. Most of the robots retreated in confusion.

Claude hit the floor with his knees bent under him. Like two enormous springs, they absorbed most of the jolt of the impact, and he rolled forward in a somersault to take care of the rest of his momentum. He started to run toward the door, firing off his blaster at the robots who stood in his way. For an instant it looked as though he might make it out, but then a blaster beam from across the room hit him squarely in the back. With a scream of pain, he fell over forward onto the polished metal floor.

Luise and Jeanne watched the death of their relative with horror. They had all known there was a chance they'd be killed on this mission, but this brought that possibility into hideous reality. At first, they were afraid that the blaster bolt might have gone straight through his body and killed Bur-Bur too; but then they saw the little brown-furred creature climbing out of the front of Claude's jumpsuit, apparently none the worse for the incident. It stood up on its hind legs for one second, gauging direction with difficulty, then dashed off at top speed out the correct door and into the hallway beyond. "Now let's just hope he finds his way out in time." Luise said grimly.

"If anyone can find their way out, it's a ticklemouse," Jeanne told her. "Besides, the robots won't be looking for anything that size, so they wouldn't even try to stop him. They'll be too busy shooting at us."

The robots in the doorways were increasing their numbers by the minute. As the word got around the castle that the last two invaders were trapped in the Chamber of Angles, reinforcements kept arriving. For every machine the two women incapacitated, another two seemed to take its place.

Slowly, playing for time now, the SOTE agents backed up the ramp. They gave no thought to getting out of the castle now; all their hopes in that direction were riding on the back of a frightened ticklemouse. All they were trying to do at the moment was stay alive until Duke Etienne and the forces of SOTE could come to their rescue.

The door through which they had originally come opened up and another robot appeared behind them. Jeanne sensed it and shouted a warning, giving Luise the opportunity to whirl and fire in this new direction. Her beam struck true and blasted a hole in the robot—but not before a bolt from the other's gun grazed the side of her right calf. The leg gave out under her and she stumbled. Were it not for Jeanne's quick action, she would have fallen to the ground with pain, but the Circus's animal trainer managed to swoop in and lend her shoulder as support. Luise leaned on her gratefully.

"I think we'd better go back out here," Jeanne said, leading Luise toward the open door at the top of the ramp. "I think there was only that one robot up there—though more will be coming soon."

As they had hoped, the upper corridor was still clear. The robots behind them were now racing up the ramp after them as Luise and Jeanne staggered across the hall back into the security room. The dead bodies of Duke Fyodor and Dr. Rustin were lying where they'd fallen, still untouched. Jeanne closed the room's door behind them as they entered and slipped the bolt shut.

"That won't keep them out," Luise gasped through her pain. "They'll blast away at it until they knock it in, then they'll be coming for us. We'd better try getting back into the dumbwaiter—we might have some chance there."

But before they could carry through on that action, they felt the entire castle shake from the force of an explosion. There was more noise and confusion out in the hall, and suddenly there were no robots trying to get in at them. They had all gone off to guard against a new menace.

"I think," Luise said, tired and hurt, "the rest of our troops have finally landed."

That was, indeed, the case. Immediately upon hearing the signal of Luise's bleeper—now outside the castle walls —Duke Etienne d'Alembert had mobilized his troops. The waiting perod had been abnormally long, and he'd been beginning to fear the worst. Now the time had come for action, and a d'Alembert never passed up such an opportunity.

The Duke had used his authority to order a small army of personnel and equipment from the local branch of SOTE. Now, at his command, they all swung into action. First came the copters, five of them, each one armed with lasers and carrying a small bomb. In one synchronized swoop, they dived at the front entrance to Rimskor Castle

131

and cracked open the gate with their simultaneously timed blasts.

Before the castle's beleaguered defenders could turn around and face the menace from this new direction, an army of fighting SOTE operatives came charging down the road toward the now opened gateway. The heavy-duty blasters that had been mounted over the doorway were dead, and the guards inside were either dead or too stunned to activate the minefield along the road bed. The Duke's legions went through the ranks of the defenders almost as if the latter weren't there. In desperation, the robot guards radioed up to the security control room for instructions, hoping to get some coordination of their efforts. But they received no answer; the only two people alive inside that control room could not work the console, and would not have helped the defenders even if they could.

Without any strategy or coordinated effort, the outnumbered robots of the late Duke Fyodor put up hardly any fight worthy of that name. Within fifteen minutes after Duke Etienne gave the order for his troops to move in, the guards surrendered to his superior forces.

As the Circus manager strode triumphantly through the corridors, he came across the body of his third-nephew Claude. He let tears fall unabashedly from his eyes at the loss of so good a man.

Luise and Jeanne appeared on the ramp above him, also looking down at Claude's charred corpse. "He died a good death," Luise said hoarsely. "If any death can be described as good. If it weren't for him, none of us would be alive now—and the information we have would be totally lost."

They walked down the ramp to him, with Luise leaning heavily on Jeanne's shoulder. As they reached the bottom, they both embraced him passionately, letting all the accumulated tension drain out of them. Etienne held onto them as long as they needed him, and then the three of them set out in search of Rick.

They found the wrestler still unconscious from a stun-gun beam and lying on a table in one of the secondary dining rooms. He probably would be all right once the initial stun wore off.

As they walked back outside, Luise briefed Etienne on what they had learned from Duke Fyodor and his physician. The head of the d'Alembert clan swore furiously under his breath when he learned that they had been aiming at the wrong goal all this time, and he was just as frustrated as Luise at not having learned more details about the other robots that were apparently on the loose throughout the Galaxy. This was a threat that had never before been suspected, and one that the Head should be apprised of immediately.

The Duke left Rimskor at once to return to the Circus, but Jeanne and Luise stayed behind for a while. As Luise watched, Jeanne went outside the castle and stood in the middle of the now darkened roadway. The young animal trainer remained rigidly motionless in the chilly night air for five minutes, then began trilling softly in an almost birdlike call. She continued on for another ten minutes, then suddenly knelt and picked something up. As she returned to Luise's side, the leader of the assault team could see that she held Bur-Bur cuddled securely in both hands. The ticklemouse's nose was twitching actively; it had come through the campaign with nary a scratch.

The instant he returned to his office at the Circus, Duke Etienne sat down at his desk and composed two coded messages. One of them was quite long, explaining in detail everything that had taken place during their operations on Kolokov and warning of the possibility of other humanoid robots elsewhere in the Empire; that message would be beamed to the Head on a Class Nine Priority basis—information vital to the continued security of the Galaxy.

The second message was shorter. It said, in effect, "Stop looking for time bombs and start looking for robots." It, too, was given a Class Nine priority and was sent out at once to the planet Ansegria.

When that message was received, its high-priority rating —the highest ever received on that particular world—got it delivered immediately to the planetary chief. But that worthy did not read it; the particular coding on it told him that the contents were not meant for his eyes and instructed him to forward it, instead, to Crown Princess Edna herself, staying with the Baron and Baroness of Cambria.

The chief delivered the message personally to Rockhold Castle. The Princess greeted him properly, though her manner was somewhat aloof; things had not been going well, and her nerves were near the fraying point. She took the message from him and dismissed him with her deepest thanks. Then, when she was sure she was alone, she summoned Jules and Yvette to her rooms. Together, they would read this important message aloud—and perhaps it would unravel some of the mystery that had overtaken the Progress.

Chapter 12

A Traitor Unmasked

".A robot!" Yvette exclaimed. "No wonder all our investigations were looking so pointless—we were going after the wrong thing. We could have been chasing time bombs from here to Doomsday while, unbeknownst to us, a machine would have been waltzing off with Edna."

The Crown Princess shuddered. "Whichever one it is must be awfully convincing," she said. "They all look like real people to me."

"Borov was, at least," Yvette said grimly. "He proved that the hard way."

"This explains a lot of mysterious things," Jules put in, pacing about the room. "It explains the fight we had in the corridor—that kick to the chest I gave him should have killed an ordinary man. And his reflexes were as quick as ours because they were mechanical and computer-assisted. And he acted as though he could see in the dark because he probably could; I know if I were making a robot traitor, I'd build a few extra features like that into it."

"Like superstrength?" Yvette gave him a wan smile.

"Exactly. That machine must be incredibly strong. That's how it uprooted the tree and clobbered poor Borov with it. Borov must have come upon it unexpectedly and learned its secret; it had to kill him to protect its identity."

"But which one of our little friends is it?" Yvette mused. "Luise wasn't able to find that out for us, unfortunately."

"So we have to use our own brains," her brother said, pacing some more. "Choyen Liu looks to me like the most logical choice. There's always something cold and emotionless about him, like a machine. He didn't sunburn like the rest of us did after that first day at the beach. And remember how good he was with that rifle on the hunt—bringing down a panna-cat like that with one shot is a pretty incredible feat."

"But remember how he calmed the dorvats when they were panicking?" Yvette countered. "I don't think a robot would be able to get so attuned to animals. And Liu wasn't the only one who didn't burn—the sun left Paul Symond untouched as well."

Crown Princess Edna felt left out of this brainstorming session as she watched the two superagents tossing their ideas back and forth. Clearing her throat, she dared to interrupt with an idea of her own. "Why don't you simply X-ray everybody and find out, instead of playing detective games?"

The two d'Alemberts stared at her. Jules stopped his pacing and smacked his forehead with his palm. *"Mon Dieu!* I must have left my brains back on DesPlaines. Edna, you are a genius, and you'll make the best Empress we've ever had." He grabbed her by both shoulders and delivered a passionate kiss to her imperial lips.

Edna was startled, but not complaining at all. When Jules had finished she blinked a little and said, "Thank you, but I'm not sure I deserve the praise. It was a simple, perfectly obvious move."

"It sometimes takes a genius to see the obvious and the simple," Yvette said solemnly. "We could both have played Sherlock Holmes all day without getting anywhere. Hm. X-raying isn't quite the answer; the machinery needed is too bulky and our robot may get suspicious as to why we need it. He knows that sort of thing would give him away in a second. He's already scared because events aren't going according to his plan; if he gets any more anxious, he may do something unpredictable. We have to avoid that."

"We've still got our own bomb detectors," Jules pointed out. "They're so small that nobody yet has noticed us using them. They should be able to detect whether a person is flesh and bone or gear and cog. We just never thought to use them on people before."

"True," Yvette nodded. "We could do that this afternoon. But we'd better plan ahead. What'll we do when we find out who it is?"

The question was harder to answer than it sounded. This robot had already proved itself to be capable and resourceful. It was not above using murder to cover its tracks, and it was already dedicated to a treasonous cause. Once its identity was revealed, it would stop at nothing to cause as much damage as it could. It had only ceased its fight with them in the corridor because it was afraid its identity might be discovered if it lingered there much longer; once that threat was no longer valid, the two agents knew just how hard a time they would have overcoming it.

"One thing is certain," Jules said. "Edna had better be far away from here when it happens."

"Absolutely," his sister agreed. "She's been sticking around so far because we had to allay our traitor's suspicions. Now that we know what his game is, there's no sense puting her in further danger. Edna, you talk to the Baron and find some way of getting out of here without anyone noticing you're gone. If anything comes up, you'll be officially sick and resting in your room."

Edna smiled at her two bodyguards. "Normally I might resent having to take orders instead of give them," she said, "but I know you two too well. Anything you say goes."

"Good," Jules said. "Now, to plan the trap itself."

Most of the candidates were assembled in the day room of Rockhold Castle, much as they had been on the day Jules had arrived. Jules mingled among them, and Jacques Roumenier stood guard beside the outer door. Though his stance appeared casual, his right hand just happened to be resting only a centimeter or so from the handle of his blaster, which he could draw and fire in the meagerest fraction of a second. Jules and Yvette had decided to use blasters if needed, since a stunner would be of no use whatsoever against a robot.

Yvette and Yvonne were waiting out of sight in the next room. Both ladies had their weapons already drawn, and were prepared to use them the instant it became necessary. The Roumeniers had been briefed on the seriousness of the threat, and would do whatever was needed to stop the robot's schemes.

137

Neither Symond nor Liu were in the room yet, so Jules took the opportunity to run a routine scan on the rest of the possibilities. As he and Yvette had suspected, they checked out to be clean and certifiably human—which left the two prime suspects unaccounted for.

Liu came in through one door at almost the same instant that Symond came in from another. They went to opposite corners of the room; Liu to meditate as always and Symond to chat with Sean Mulvaney.

Jules decided to try Liu first. Going over to the man, he said in a quiet voice that only the two of them could hear, "Something's been puzzling me about you."

"Oh?" The Anarian looked up at him, an expressionless expression on his face.

"Yes. When I first met you I mentioned that you had a very strong grip for such a frail-looking person as yourself, and you answered by saying that the Universe was full of illusion and that no one is ever quite what he seems. What did you mean by that?"

As he spoke, Jules used his sensors to try to probe the Anarian's body. One sensor was in his ring, the other in his belt buckle. Both were reading normal. Liu was not a robot.

"There are as many levels to reality as there are to illusion," the Anarian answered. "I have the humble ability to see past certain illusions, though sometimes the entire reality eludes me. I know, for instance, that you are not what you pretend to be."

Jules was shaken. "How do you know that?"

"Your physique, your bone structure when I shook your hand—they are not characteristic of one who comes from a normal gravity world, such as you purport to. Also, I am quite familiar with galactography and current politics, and I know there is no such planet named Julea."

"If you knew that was so, why didn't you unmask me as a fraud?"

"Illusion serves its part in reality. To destroy illusion without understanding its reason for being is to act unwisely."

"Is there anyone else here who is also an illusion?" Jules asked. He wanted to test Liu's powers of observation to see whether the Anarian had come to the same conclusion as himself.

"Yes," Liu answered calmly. "We all are, even me. In a situation of pressure like this, we all project an idealized version of ourselves, a composite of our dreams and our ideals, our aspirations and our fears." He paused. "There is, however, one who is more illusion than the rest."

"Who is it, and in what way?" Jules prodded.

Choyen Liu looked at him with eyes whose depths Jules could not begin to plumb. "Must you ask me to tell you what you already know? You should not ask a teacher to be a parrot."

Jules bowed his head in acknowledgement of the point. Despite the oddness of the man, he was beginning to like Choyen Liu. Somehow, the Anarian knew more than he could possibly see, and told even less than he saw. "You're right," he said. "Forgive me."

But if Choyen Liu was not the robot, that meant it had to be Paul Symond. Symond, the handsome, friendly, outgoing young man whom everybody liked. Symond, the personable chap who made such pleasant conversation and such a trustworthy confidant. Symond, the traitor.

Who better to snare a princess? Jules thought bitterly.

Still, he had to make absolutely certain of his hypothesis before condemning Symond to death—or whatever the equivalent of death was for a machine. Walking with forced casualness over to the other side of the room, he stood for a moment beside Symond as the candidate was talking to Mulvaney. The sensors he was wearing showed no doubt at all, though—Symond was a machine in human form. Jules gave a slight nod of his head to indicate to Jacques that this was the one they wanted.

The problem now was to get Symond away from the rest of the candidates; Jules didn't want anyone else hurt if it could be avoided. "Paul," he said quietly, "I wonder if I could talk to you privately for a moment."

Maybe it was something in the tone of Jules's voice, or the particular posture in which he was standing. Maybe Jacques made his move a trifle too soon toward his blaster, or looked at Symond with a little too much anxiety. Maybe it was a combination of any or all of those factors. But whatever it was, something alerted the robot to the fact that his identity was now known. His brain assimilated that information in a flash and knew that he would never have a chance to accomplish his mission now—and with

139

that realization, the second overwhelming drive of his being took over: survival. Survival at all costs.

Without giving the slightest warning, he lashed out with both hands at both Jules and Mulvaney. The latter was knocked halfway across the room and lost consciousness as his head banged roughly against the wall; but Jules was a little harder to get rid of.

The blow, coming as unexpectedly as it did, stunned him and pushed him backward a few awkward steps. But he did not lose his balance, nor did he bump into anything. All the blow really accomplished was to gain Symond a few vital seconds.

At the same instant the robot lashed out at the two men around him, he started running. As quick as Jacques was at drawing his blaster, by the time he had it out of its holster and ready to fire the treacherous machine was halfway across the room and on the other side of a knot of other candidates. Those men, too confused by this sudden activity, just stood dumbstruck in the middle of the room, effectively blocking Jacques's aim. The SOTE agent's reverence for innocent human life made him hesitate one instant before pressing the trigger on his gun —and in that instant, Symond was out the door into the adjoining room.

Yvette and Yvonne had been waiting in this room for something to happen, blasters drawn and at the ready. But so quickly did Symond come bursting through the door, with no warning whatsoever, that they barely had time to react. It would be hard to say who was the more surprised at this confrontation—Symond at finding two more armed people waiting for him or the SOTE agents at having him appear so unexpectedly. But Symond, with his computer-fast reflexes, recovered first.

He now knew that he was in the most crucial fight of his short existence, and was not about to pull any punches as he'd done in the corridor battle. Yvette was standing nearest him, on his left, and he lashed out with the flat of his left hand aimed directly at her throat. It was a blow of killing ferocity, and so quickly did it come that Yvette was not able to duck. Her DesPlainian reflexes were quick enough, however, to cause her to fall backwards even as the blow was being delivered. Symond's hand, therefore, caught her with slightly less than its intended impact; it did not break her neck, and the toughened muscles in her throat prevented the blow from shattering her windpipe. But she was knocked, senseless, to the floor and lay still for several minutes before regaining consciousness.

That left Vonnie to deal with. The attack on Yvette had given her a precious second in which to bring her blaster into play. It was not just because she was his fiancée that Jules had picked her for this assignment; on the 1,000-point test by which all SOTE agents were measured—a test of both mental and physical agility—she had scored a highly respectable 989. There were perhaps only two dozen other people in the Galaxy with a higher rating than that.

But no one could have predicted just how quickly Symond could act. No living being had a right to move so fast and so effectively, not even a DesPlainian—but, of course, Symond was not a living being. His computerized brain could assess a situation and react to it more quickly than could a human one. His body parts were purely mechanical, and were not subject to haphazard impulses, as were human tissue. When he moved, there was no hesitation, no infinitesimal delay between thought and deed. Even to Yvonne's well-trained eyes, Symond came at her as a mere blur of motion.

She had time to fire just one shot, which passed through the space right behind the quick-moving robot. Then Symond had reached her. One of his powerful fists pounded brutally into her stomach and, as she doubled over involuntarily, his other came down with savage force on the back of her neck. Yvonne fell to the floor, unconscious.

All the while—unhampered by emotions, adrenalin, or any of the other distractions that would overtake a living being in similar circumstances—Symond's computer brain was evaluating his chances for survival. Success lay in flight, but even that course was fraught with peril. There were no copters on the premises, and trying to escape on the back of a dorvat would be ludicrous. That left a car as the only logical alternative. But in a car he would be alone and unable to fight back; they could spot him from the air and simply drop a bomb on him, and that would be the end of everything. He could not allow that to happen.

There was one other tack he could try. If he took a hostage with him, they might not bomb him. It might make them think twice before destroying him. A hostage would be his leverage to pry loose his continued safety. He could only take one, because two might be hard to manage if he had to fight, and he was limited to what was at hand—but women always did make exceptionally good hostages. Humans seemed to have a built-in bias to protect them at all costs.

All these thoughts were flashing through his mind even as he was approaching Yvonne. Consequently, he held back a trifle and his blows merely knocked her out rather than kill her. Before her body could slump completely to the floor, he had swooped her up in one arm and hoisted her over his shoulder. Without the slightest slackening in his speed, he flashed through the room and carried his unconscious bundle into the hallway beyond and out the front door of Rockhold Castle.

It was only a second or so later that Jules raced into the room where the two women had been waiting. His eyes surveyed the scene and instantly spotted the stricken body of his sister. Kneeling beside her, he checked quickly for a pulse, and emitted a grateful sigh of relief to find that it was still there. With that fear allayed, he looked around the room for some sign of his fiancée, just as Jacques rushed through the door.

"Look after Evie," Jules snapped to his friend. There was no clue to Vonnie's whereabouts, which could only mean one thing—Symond had taken her with him. And that meant Jules's girl friend was either unconscious or dead, because Jules knew that, were she conscious, she would have been struggling too hard for even the robot to handle.

Leaving his sister to Jacques's able care, Jules ran through the castle to the courtyard where the cars were parked just in time to see Symond driving off through the front gate with a body slumped in the seat beside him—a body that could only be Yvonne Roumenier.

Chapter 13

The Chase in Space

Though his soul was in agony over Vonnie's possible fate, Jules was not the sort to stop and moan about the situation. He was a creature of action, and every cell in his body called out for him to take steps to remedy the situation. Without wasting a single tear, he bounded down the front steps to where his own car was parked. It was the work of but a second to hop in the front seat and start the engine, and then he was zooming down the road and out the front gate himself, in hot pursuit of the traitor's car.

Jules's own vehicle was something special in the way of groundcars. While it looked to the casual observer like a late sports model Frascati, it was actually a Mark Forty-One Service Special. It was ever so slightly longer, wider, and rounder than a car of its class should be—and it was considerably heavier. For its size it was the most efficient and deadly vehicle ever built. At the touch of a button, those too-round sides would open and a transparent, airtight, beamproof canopy would slide into place around the car. It could fly through the air or even short distances into space and accelerate up, forward, back, or sideways at better than four gees. Its communication gear was complete in every respect, and it was fully armed with heavy-duty blasters and a variety of bombs.

But all that expensive and elaborate equipment did Jules no good at all in the present circumstances; he still dared not use it against the car ahead of him. Not while Vonnie was in it.

Symond drove his car at the limit on manual, relying on his own super-reflexes to keep him safely on the road. Jules's reflexes were certainly not much worse, and he was able to keep up the chase without mishap. He could have, if he chose, taken off and flown above the escaping vehicle, but that might have been tipping his hand a bit prematurely—plus, there would be complications on landing once the other vehicle stopped. For the moment, Jules preferred to stay on the road and take his chances in the traffic.

But that is not to say he was idle during the drive. Even as he steered his groundcar along the highway in pursuit of his quarry, he was on the radio to Service Headquarters for Ansegria. Using a top-level code, he identified himself as Agent Wombat—and did that name ever produce results! Agents Wombat and Periwinkle (Yvette) were almost legendary in Service annals, and a request from either was like a direct order from the Head himself. So when Jules asked for a tracer placed on Symond's fleeing groundcar plus an escort of copters to make sure it didn't get away, he got exactly that—and fast.

No attempt was made to disguise the surveillance forces being used against the renegade robot, but if Symond noticed the copters at all he paid them no attention. He was positive they would take no direct action against him while he still had his hostage; his problem was still the same as it had been all along—to escape from the planet. Once he was in space, he would have a much better chance of eluding pursuit and finding a safe haven.

It soon became evident to all the pursuers that Symond's groundcar was headed via back-country roads to Canyonville, where the local spaceport was located. The idea of placing roadblocks in his path was suggested, but Jules vetoed it out of hand. As long as Symond was no direct threat to the Princess, he felt they should let the traitor have some leeway in the hope that he would slip and give them a chance to rescue Yvonne unhurt. Once his fiancée was out of danger, Jules didn't care what happened to the traitor.

As predicted, Symond's car drove up to the spaceport and did a quick circle of the field while the robot scouted the possibilities. Finally, spotting a small mail ship sitting on its fins in one corner of the field, the robot drove his

144

groundcar in a beeline straight for it. He stopped alongside the untended ship and got out of his car. Carrying the still unconscious Yvonne over his shoulder, he began climbing the ladder to the ship's crew section.

Jules felt a moment of frustration as his own car raced over to the mail ship. For just an instant, Symond was visible and vulnerable; yet the blasters in Jules's car were heavy-duty ones that would destroy everything in the area they hit. He would not be able to shoot the robot without hitting Vonnie as well. He cautioned the pilots of the copters not to try any sniping with their hand weapons, either; the copters made an unreliable shooting base, and there was the chance they might hit the wrong target. Besides, hitting Symond once he had started up the ladder meant he would have dropped Vonnie to the ground in his fall— and that could be fatal.

The SOTE forces could only watch, helpless, as Symond reached the top of the ladder with his captive and disappeared inside the airlock, closing it behind him. Jules wasn't sure whether there were any crewmembers or not inside that ship, but it wouldn't make too much difference. A vessel that small could be handled easily enough by one person who knew what he was doing, which Symond probably did.

Jules checked with the Service officers about the possibility of getting Navy or police ships to head Symond off. But Ansegria was a small and quiet planet that had never had much trouble it couldn't handle itself; its police didn't have anything more advanced than atmospheric jets. The Navy occasionally sent a fleet ship over on holidays or special occasions, but in general the nearest base was over a parsec away. If Symond ever did get off the ground, both the Service and the local police would have an impossible time trying to catch him.

Which meant that everything lay on Jules's shoulders. Gunning his car at maximum acceleration, he zoomed across the spaceport field to his and Yvette's own vessel, *La Comète Cuivré*. The burnished metal of the sleek two-person ship glowed almost red in the late afternoon sunlight. At the touch of one special button on his car's control panel, a section of the *Comet's* hull opened downward, forming a ramp that the car could drive straight up. The Mark Forty-One Service Special snugged perfectly into the hold of the ship and the ramp closed up behind it, sealing it airtight.

Even before the hull had completely closed, though, Jules had leaped out of the driver's seat of his car and begun climbing the ladder up to the forward section of the ship. Within seconds he was in the familiar control cabin of his own ship, seated before the console. The *Comet* was in a powered-down configuration, as he had not been expecting to use it during the course of this mission; consequently, he had to work furiously, flipping switches and turning dials in an effort to get the vessel ready for a leap into space.

Slowly, the atomic reactors that powered the *Comet* began to glow as life returned to the ship. The drive circuits heated up nicely to the point where they could be called upon when needed. Jules gave all the indicators a check with an experienced eye, and everything read perfect. The *Comet* was ready to fly whenever he gave the order.

Jules radioed SOTE and had them inform the tower that his wishes were to supersede all other normal business. He then issued the order that regular departures and arrivals were to be held until this matter concerning the hijacked mail ship was settled. If Symond and he had to take off on short notice, he didn't want either of them colliding with another ship in midair.

The robot obviously had not found too much opposition inside the mail ship, for it suddenly lifted off the launch field with a blaze of acceleration that made most onlookers gasp. No normal human would have taken off so hard; he wouldn't have been able to work the delicate controls for very long under such heavy gee forces, and might have passed out, which would have been fatal. Jules set his lower jaw and tracked the stolen ship on his radar screen. It was leaving the surface of Ansegria at a rate of about six gravities; well, that would not be too bad. To someone from a three-gee world, six gees would be little more than an inconvenience.

As the mail ship blasted its way through Ansegria's sky, Jules's ship followed right after it, matching speed for speed. Jules wondered whether Symond speculated on what sort of pilot could be withstanding that great an acceleration for so long, but then realized that the robot must already have some measure of his worth—that fight in the corridor had taught the robot as much about Jules as it had taught Jules about the robot. Each knew fairly well the capabilities of his adversary.

The acceleration didn't slacken at all as the two ships left Ansegria's atmosphere behind them. Symond apparently didn't want to waste an instant reaching a distance far enough from Ansegria's gravitational field to turn on his subether drive and escape to some other system. Jules was just as determined not to give him that opportunity.

Upping his own acceleration to eight gees, Jules closed the gap between the two ships. When they were but half a kilometer apart, the SOTE agent brought his weapons to bear on the other's vessel. Jules had been waiting for Symond to make his mistake, and now the robot had made two of them—he had trapped himself in a vehicle that could be effectively disabled without being destroyed, and he had hijacked one that was unarmed. That combination would—Jules prayed fervently—prove the traitor's undoing.

Taking careful aim, Jules fired the *Comet's* blasters full strength at the tail of the fugitive's ship. These were not hand blasters, whose beams could be stopped by a tough enough metal alloy; these were high-powers, and there was little that could withstand their full fury. The rear end of Symond's ship began heating up; it glowed first a cherry red, then graduated to white hot. With a suddenness that only seemed to happen in space, the back part of the fleeing vessel burst apart in a silent explosion, scattering bits of debris into orbit around Ansegria. At the same time, the ship's acceleration stopped abruptly and the rocket began coasting through space at the steady speed it had had at the moment just before its engines blew.

Jules noted quickly that he had acted in time; the ship would not reach subether distance from Ansegria for another two hours. That allowed him plenty of time; the matter would be settled between Symond and himself, one way or another, long before that point was reached.

For the next few minutes, though, he was very busy decelerating, making sure that his own ship didn't overshoot his quarry. Matching velocities was considered a routine procedure, and was something that every pilot-in-training was required to master before obtaining his license;

nevertheless, it was detailed and it took a good deal of time before Jules could adjust his speed and direction to exactly parallel that of the disabled ship.

With that accomplished, Jules set grimly about his task of putting on a suit of space armor. Matching velocities with the mail ship may have been a laborious and tedious procedure, but it was a much preferable pastime to boarding a disabled ship with a berserk robot loose on it.

Jules left the airlock of the *Comet* and floated across the void to the stricken ship. The airlock would not open at his command, but he had expected that; Symond was not about to open the door for him, as it were. Nevertheless, there were ways to get around that difficulty.

Jules looked around for a second until he found the emergency manual controls, which could override instructions from the bridge. Symond had intentionally left the airlock's inner door open, so Jules's first order of business was to close that before he could open the outer door. The manual crank did not want to turn at first—Jules surmised that the robot had propped the inner door open with something—but, using all his strength, Jules forced it to start its work. In a matter of seconds he had closed it and begun the pumping procedure for emptying the air out of the chamber. The mail ship's failsafe system would not let the inner door open again until Jules was ready to let it.

When all the air was out of the lock, Jules opened the outer door and stepped inside the ship. Closing the hatch behind him, he began the tedious procedure for letting the air back into the lock. Even when there was an atmosphere around him, though, he did not remove his space armor. Although Symond's chest expanded and contracted at regular intervals, Jules doubted very much whether the robot really needed to breathe. As a last resort, the creature could always knock a hole in the airlock door to let the air out of the ship, and if Jules were not encased in his own suit it would be a quick way to end the opposition. Jules would not give Symond such an easy way out.

As the inner door opened, Jules noted that all the lights inside the ship had been turned off. That, too, was as he had anticipated. The robot had already demonstrated his ability to see in the dark; it would be to his advantage to keep Jules as far off balance as he could. The SOTE agent calmly reached up to the top of his helmet and switched on its high-intensity searchlight beam. If Symond insisted on playing games like this, Jules would top him; anyone now coming face to face with him would be staring directly into that dazzling light, and Jules doubted whether even the robot could see through that much glare.

Jules found himself in a corridor that ran fore to aft along the axis of the ship. The most likely place for the robot to be was in the front of the vessel, in the control room were he could monitor and control what happened inside the hijacked rocket. With grim determination he began swimming through the hallway toward the bridge.

The beam of his searchlight gave a harsh effect to the interior of the darkened vessel. Objects directly in front of him reflected strongly, while deep shadows and blackness ringed the periphery of his vision. Jules knew he was an exposed target as he swam down the center of the corridor in free-fall, but the thought didn't bother him too much. Symond had used a stun-gun against him in the corridor of Rockhold Castle the other night, but such a weapon would be useless against him when he was encased in space armor. There was no indication that the robot had any armament more powerful than that; and, even if he had, Jules's armor could withstand the full fury of most hand-held weapons except for the highest powered blasters. And Jules's own blaster was in his hand and at the ready for instant use should he catch sight of his quarry.

The door to the front compartment was closed, meaning that some surprise was obviously awaiting him in there. The door could be opened by sliding it upward into the top of the doorsill. Floating up to the very top, Jules reached over to press the button that would open the door, fully expecting Symond to have it locked. To his surprise, it slid open easily, and he gazed in to see what was inside.

He had only a brief glimpe. Vonnie was floating toward the front of the cabin, still unconscious. Several lights on the control panel were quietly shining, and one red light was flickering on and off most urgently—obviously the automatic monitor from the aft compartment telling the captain that the engines were blown and that the drive chamber was open to the vacuum of space. Symond was not in the room.

Before Jules had more than the merest flash of that sight, however, a massive object hit him hard along the side of his helmet. The battle armor was sturdy and was little more than dented by the blow—but even so, the impact was so great that it drove him forward against the bulkhead. His helmet banged hard against the metal wall, setting up a ringing in his ears. Even though stunned, Jules's rapid DesPlainian reflexes enabled him to twist his body around to see where the attack had come from.

Symond had been waiting in the back of the corridor all along, figuring that Jules would head straight for the control room. He had sneaked up soundlessly behind the SOTE operative, waiting for the perfect moment to attack. When Jules's attention had been focused on the interior of the bridge, Symond had picked up some massive metallic object and hurled it, with all his superhuman strength, at his adversary. Then, not bothering to wait to see how much damage that would do, he launched himself directly after it.

Jules struggled valiantly to fight off the stunning effects of the blow on the head as he saw Symond's body come hurtling through the air at him. He brought up his right arm to fire his blaster but, fast as he was, he was still a fraction of a second too late. The robot's body banged solidly into his, bumping him once more against the bulkhead. Symond's hand gripped that of Jules and squeezed with unbelievable power. The blaster, a sturdy amalgam of plastic and steel, crumbled as though it had been made of cardboard. The situation, then, seemed to resolve itself down to basics—a DesPlainian human of supernormal capabilities and a humanoid robot of mechanical perfection.

Symond had the initial advantage and intended to press it for all it was worth. With his right hand he pounded Jules again and again in the stomach; the blows reached the agent's midsection as though delivered by a pile driver. His body armor was well constructed to withstand a large variety of abuses, but it could not outlast such punishing treatment for long without breaking apart. Jules would have to do something to keep Symond's hands too busy to continue that work.

Fighting in free-fall is almost entirely a matter of leverage; sheer physical strength is of secondary consequence when every action produces an equal and opposite reaction and there is no firm place to stand. As long as Jules remained pressed up against the bulkhead, Symond's punches

150

would have a telling effect; if he were free in midair, the blows would not be nearly so bad.

With his right leg, he lashed out sideways and kicked against the wall. His kick was strong enough to break him free of the robot's grasp and send him sailing down the corridor. He would probably have sailed all the way to the back of the ship if he'd let himself, but that would not have done any good. Instead, he reached out to grab a doorsill as he passed it, and stopped his motion. As his head cleared from the initial attack, he began to feel some of his energy being renewed.

Pushing himself off from this door, he headed back toward his foe. Symond saw him coming and braced himself against the frame of the doorway, but there was little he could do against the inertia of Jules's hundred-kilo body hitting him squarely in the midsection. The two antagonists tumbled over and over through the air into the center of the control room.

Jules looked beyond his opponent for a second. Yvonne appeared to be coming to from the blow Symond had given her. The thought of having her as his ally against the treacherous humanoid machine sent a little spark of hope through his body. He and Vonnie made almost as unbeatable a team as he and Yvette.

But Yvonne was not fully conscious yet, and Jules would have to keep Symond from realizing that she was snapping out of her coma. The robot had already proved that he could fight effectively against two opponents at once; only if he was unaware of Yvonne's presence would she be a true asset.

Jules began raining random blows down upon the robot's head, forcing him to go on the defensive and making sure his eyes stayed focused on Jules. The SOTE agent tried not to look over to his fiancée too often, for his eyes would give her away. He concentrated instead on being a nuisance to Symond.

Yvonne, meanwhile, came around slowly. Being in free-fall tended to confuse her, adding the sinking stomach sensation to the confusion normally attendant on returning to consciousness from a blow on the head. Everything around her was dark except for one light bobbing around in front of her. Her brain was swimming in dizziness, and she tried

151

to focus on the light to clear it. After a moment, she succeeded.

The light was on the top of a suit of space armor, and she recognized it instantly as Jules's. No one else had a body shape like that, or moved in quite that way. Yvonne had made herself an expert on the subject of Jules d'Alembert, and could recognize him instantly in any disguise he chose.

He was fighting—very poorly, for him—a dark, shadowy figure whom she could only see from the back. It took just an instant for the recognition to click in her mind, and then she knew it was Symond. But where were they? Why were they in the control room of a spaceship? How had they gotten out into space at all? Where were Yvette and Jacques?

She shoved those and a host of other questions to the back of her mind. This was a time for action, not for riddles. Jules was fighting a very dangerous traitor, and he needed her help.

As she watched, she could see that Jules was doing a very bad job of attacking. Although he was engaged in many furious motions, the waste of effort was incredible. Then she realized what his intention was—he was keeping Symond's back to her, not letting the robot know she was now an active force. She would have the advantage of surprise—but how best to use it?

Hitting Symond would do little good; the creature was close to indestructible. What would stop it? Her brain raced in feverish circles for fifteen seconds before the obvious answer occurred to her, and it took another couple of instants to figure out how to carry out her plan quickly and quietly. The instant she reasoned it out, however, she carried through.

She knew something about the way control panels were constructed. There were always plenty of backup systems in case something should go wrong. And, although most of the electronic circuits were printed on circuitboard, there would be auxiliary power lines fed into the board by cables. Floating slowly, so that Symond's peripheral vision wouldn't spot her motion, she made her way down to the panel. The pair of cables were there, as she expected, soldered tightly into place. There was no gentle means of disconnecting them, and she didn't have time for such methods anyhow.

152

Using brute, DesPlainian strength, she pulled the cables free of their moorings and held them by the insulation. Then, judging her direction very carefully, she leaped at Symond.

The robot saw her coming out of the corner of his eye, but there was little he could do—Jules had coordinated his attack to what he saw Yvonne doing, and Symond was already in midmotion to block one of Jules's punches. As he twisted away, he ran right into the two outstretched tips of cable that Yvonne was poking at him.

There was a loud crackling sound and sparks filled the room. Just as Yvonne had thought, electrocution was the perfect method for dealing with this robot. The power flowing through the ship's cables had overwhelmed the creature's own circuitry, burning it out. The robot's carcass twitched spasmodically until Yvonne removed the cables and pushed them to one side; then it lay still, floating lifeless in midair.

Through Jules's helmet she could just make out an enormous smile of relief on his face. He swam over to her, put his arms around her not-so-frail body, and began to hug her passionately.

"Darling," she cried out, "I enjoy hugging you, too—but please remove your armor first! It's no fun at all this way!"

Chapter 14

The Iceberg's Tip

Ideally, all the d'Alemberts would have preferred to have their funerals on their native planet, DesPlaines; but that was impossible. The Circus of the Galaxy was too big and too complex to be able to shut down whenever one of its members was killed in the line of duty. Besides, it had a cover identity to protect. It could not even officially admit that anyone *had* died, lest too many questions be asked about how and why the death had occurred.

Consequently, the funerals for the four family members who had died on Kolokov—three in the raid on Evekian and Claude d'Alembert in Rimskor Castle—were almost furtive affairs. The bodies were cremated, and the ashes were sent back to DesPlaines; the services themselves were held under the big top after all the customers had departed from the last show of the evening.

Jules and Yvette, Jacques and Yvonne—their mission on Ansegria now over—had joined the Circus on Kolokov so that they could take part in the sad ceremony. They knew that, had the circumstances been a little different, the funeral could have been for them, and they felt a deep sense of personal loss over their dead kinsmen. But even so, they knew it was occasions like this that bonded the family ever stronger and closer together; the d'Alemberts would go on as long as the Empire lasted, and this renewed faith helped them face future missions ever more eagerly.

Etienne, as was his duty as head of the family, delivered

the funeral oration. As often as he had performed this sad chore, it was a new weight on his shoulders each time. He spoke quietly and with dignity, always bearing in mind the faces of the four he would be seeing no more; and when he finished, there was nothing else to be said.

He spoke to more than just the family members who were present in the room, too, for the Head himself—Grand Duke Zander von Wilmenhorst—had decided to "attend" via interstellar trivid patch-in. Although he couldn't spare the time to leave Earth, his image was projected, at great expense, all the way across the countless parsecs to a booth on Kolokov that was set out of the way so that most of the family couldn't detect his identity; and he listened most intently and reverently to the Duke's words about the departed relatives.

Afterward the trivid booth was moved into the Duke's private office, where Etienne, Jules, Yvette, and the Head could discuss the case among themselves. The Head first congratulated the three d'Alemberts on another successful mission, but Jules and Yvette demurred. It was their relatives, they pointed out, who actually broke the secret behind the plot, and it was Yvonne who actually destroyed the robot.

The Head nodded slowly. "I'm not belittling their roles in the slightest, and they'll all get a verbal pat on the head. That's all I can do; because of the ultrasecret nature of the Circus's real mission, I can't put their commendations in writing. But the three of you were in charge of the operation—and a succesful mission is a reflection on its planners. There was a threat to the Empire; I put you in charge and now that threat is gone. Ergo, you handled it well and deserve my thanks . . . and the Princess's."

"The logic still seems a bit strained," Jules said, "but on behalf of all those who worked with us, I thank you for your kind words."

"Unfortunately, though," Yvette intoned, "the threat is not gone. If what Luise learned is true—and Doctor Rustin was under nitrobarb, so it must be—then there are more robots like Symond wandering around. I figure a minimum of three, because Rustin said 'none of the others' rather than 'neither of the others.' There could be many more than that. This one was only the latest—and since there haven't been any signs of any of the others, they must be infiltrating well enough to pass inspection. Who knows where they could be by now?"

The Head's face clouded over. It was clear that this was a problem to which he had devoted a great deal of his personal attention over these past few days. "Yes," he sighed. "But we know now that these robots are not invincible—or even undetectable. Our first concern, of course, is that some of them may have slipped into positions of trust near the Imperial Family. The next most serious point would be if any of them were in the military or impersonating Service personnel.

"There is an easy enough way of checking, however. At my request, the Emperor will order all Court employees— and all Service personnel and ranking military officers—to undergo frequent health check-ups . . . including X rays. It would be easy enough to justify such an order, and it wouldn't arouse the suspicions of any robots working in those areas. It would be enough to scare them into action, though, because they know such a check-up would expose them. Either they'll panic and flee, or they'll try to perform their missions prematurely; in either case, we stand a good chance of spoiling their plans."

"But," said Duke Etienne grimly, "what if these robots aren't in any position where we can check on them directly? Statistically speaking, that's a more likely prospect."

The Head sighed again. "Yes, old friend, I know that only too well. The total population of the Empire runs into the trillions, out of which we have to pick a few select traitors. The odds are stacked improbably high against us. What if one of the robots is a janitor in some building, just awaiting his appointed hour to strike? How could we possibly spot something like that?"

"The same way we spotted this one," Yvette said, trying to project more optimism than she felt. "If they're going to do anything, they have to make a move sometime. We'll be keeping our eyes open even wider now that we know the threat exists. The Service of the Empire is the finest organization of its kind ever assembled, and our people are the sharpest and most loyal subjects the Emperor could have." I have confidence in us that we'll be able to move in time."

"Funny—Bill said the same thing in almost the same words," the Head told them, referring to the Emperor. "I respect his judgment, and I hope he's right. There is, you know, one other factor to consider. Duke Fyodor and Doctor Rustin were only parts in what had to be a widespread conspiracy."

Jules knit his brow in perplexity. "Exactly how do you figure that, sir?"

The Head looked to his friend Etienne, who shrugged his massive shoulders and spoke to his son. "Fyodor Paskoi was Duke of Kolokov. As such, he had a great deal of power on this one planet—but, theoretically, none anywhere else. Paul Symond—the original one—came from Lateesta, a different planet entirely. There had to be someone on Lateesta who knew in advance that Symond would be chosen as that world's representative to the Progress. There had to be someone who could gather the data on him so that he could be duplicated in robot form."

"Nor is that all of it," added Zander von Wilmenhorst. "There also had to be someone relatively close to the Imperial Family to be able to predict what Edna's tastes would be like, so that the robot could be designed to match them. As far as this case goes, I'm afraid, we've only seen the tip of the iceberg. We'll have to do a lot more diving beneath the surface before we can map out the entire structure of this hazard. I hope the two of you won't mind a lot more hard work in the future."

"We thrive on it!" Jules promised.

"And on the subject of Edna's tastes," Yvette said thoughtfully, "I think whoever designed the Symond robot doesn't know the way women think very well. Symond had all the obvious qualities—good looks, charming personality, sparkling wit—the whole supposedly ideal package. Edna even admitted to me she was interested in him. He's the kind of guy that most girls, including myself, would love to go on dates with . . . but I think Edna would have been too smart to marry him. You can't marry perfection. If you ask me, I think Edna's eyes are aimed in an entirely different direction."

"Where?" Jules asked.

"Choyen Liu," his sister replied without hesitation. As Jules raised his eyebrows in amazement, she went on, "I know he's not the standard romantic picture, but marriage will dissolve the ideal very quickly. Symond was all surface. Choyen Liu has no surface to speak of, but there's a

157

depth there that would take a lifetime to plumb. Edna's looking for someone to spend her lifetime with, and there's one thing I can guarantee—Choyen Liu won't be boring. I really believe she may end up marrying him."

The Head listened to Yvette, and considered the message that Edna had sent her parents earlier that very day—that there was someone she'd met on the Progress whom she was seriously considering, and she would like to talk the matter over with them when she returned home. He himself would not have thought this fellow Choyen Liu—whom he knew only through his files—would be the sort of man the Princess would pick. But then, he was not in the matchmaking business.

He smiled as the conversation continued to revolve around the Princess and her possible husband. It was not really the basic concern of any of them—Liu's file indicated that he was a good and loyal servant of the Crown, and that was what mattered as far as the Service was concerned. But his top agents needed to relax their minds before starting out again on the uphill fight against entropy. He knew beyond doubt that they would soon be risking their lives once more to maintain the ideal of Empire. In the meantime, let them enjoy some idle speculation for a bit.